praise f

"Alfau's inventive 'comedy of gestures' is, like any hall-of-mirrors fun house, disorienting, maddening and greatly entertaining. It has everything any modern best-seller needs: murder, incest, fallen priests, lascivious nuns, a couple of suicides, several mysteries, the living dead, pimps and whores and poets, locales that shift from China to the Philippines to the Caribbean to Europe."—*Washington Post*

"This is a work as much about fiction's creation of places outside time as about the antics of madmen."—*Times Literary Supplement*

"Recent readers have compared Alfau not only with Nabokov and Calvino but with García Márquez and Borges."—*New Yorker*

"A vastly satisfying book . . . I enjoyed every moment of his dark and lively tale."—*Saturday Review*

"A spectacularly original novel—witty, ingenious and haunting. It also uncannily anticipates many of the directions taken by experimental fiction since the war."—*Sunday Correspondent*

"From the outset it is clear that we are in the shadowlands between reality and fiction, where anything can happen, and usually does."—*The Independent*

books by Felipe Alfau

Locos: A Comedy of Gestures

Chromos

Sentimental Songs (La poesía cursi)

Locos

a comedy of gestures

Felipe Alfau

Afterword by Mary McCarthy

Dalkey Archive Press

Originally published by Farrar & Rinehart, Inc. 1936
Copyright © 1936, 1963 Felipe Alfau
Afterword copyright © 1988 Mary McCarthy
Corrected edition copyright © 1988 Dalkey Archive Press

Dalkey Archive Press:

First hardback edition, 1988
Second printing, 1991
First paperback edition, 1997

Library of Congress Cataloging-in-Publication Data
Alfau, Felipe, 1902-
Locos: a comedy of gestures
I. Title
PS3501.L45L6   1988   813'.52   88-14975
ISBN 1-56478-171-2

This publication is partially supported by grants from the National
Endowment for the Arts, a federal agency, and the Illinois Arts
Council, a state agency.

Dalkey Archive Press
Illinois State University
Campus Box 4241
Normal, IL 61790-4241

Contents

Prologue

THIS . . . NOVEL IS WRITTEN IN SHORT STORIES WITH THE PURPOSE OF facilitating the task of the reader. In this way the reader does not have to begin the book near a given cover and finish it at a point nearer the opposite cover. Each chapter being a complete story in itself, the reader may pick up this book and begin it at the back and end it at the front, or he may begin it and end it in the middle, depending on his mood. In other words, he can read it in any fashion except, perhaps, upside down.

However, for the benefit of those in whom the habit of reading a book in the usual manner is deeply set and painful to eradicate, the pages have been numbered clearly and the stories arranged less clearly in a conventional order which my friend, Dr. José de los Rios, and myself have found somewhat adequate.

Aside from this superficial arrangement, I am not entirely to blame for committing this novel; the characters used in it being, I believe, far more responsible than myself.

For some time I have been realizing more and more clearly the way which characters have of growing independent, of rebelling against their creator's will and command, of mocking their author, of toying with him, dragging him through some unsuspected and grotesque path all their own, often entirely contrary to that which the author has planned for them. This tendency is so marked in my characters that it makes my work most difficult and places me in many a predicament.

Such rebellious spirit is shown in these people by a strong desire to become real beings. They often steal into persons I have met and assume the most extraordinary attitudes according to what they think true life is. They assume what in persons is called a pose and has often ended a promising friendship for me. For them reality is what fiction is to real people; they simply love it and make for it against my almost heroic opposition. As one of them says:

> "Characters have visions of true life—they dream reality and then they are lost."

I should add: the author is lost.

And even as I write this prologue, I realize how true this is, for I can find no connection with that individual and official author of this book who once while in the mad, fantastic city of Toledo wandered one day with his friend, Dr. José de los Rios, into the Café de los Locos (the Café of the Crazy) where he witnessed things and saw people which in his playful imagination took the shape of this book, who with the lack of conscience typical of an author advised an acquaintance there to trade his insignificant, though real life in this world for the still less significant and not at all real existence in these pages, who at the end of a chapter flung a window open and let in real life to take the stuffy and fictional life of the one character who was his childhood friend and who in a persistent confabulation with the characters found in that Toledo café, is the abstract, but nevertheless real, perpetrator of this experiment.

The result of this is a bunch of contradictory characters inconsequent as their author and just as clumsy in their performance. As their personality is a passing and unsteady thing that lasts at most a book's length, they have lost respect for it and change it at will, because they have a faint idea that life is abrupt and unexpected.

Their knowledge of reality is vague and imprecise. Sometimes I have given a character the part of a brother or a son, and in the middle of the action he begins to make love to his sister or his mother, because he has heard that men sometimes make love to women. Another character appears as a child in a situation that takes place when he should be a mature man, because he attributes his persistent failure to understand the situation to immaturity typical of childhood. Again, another character, who has the part of a chicken, begins to bark in the middle of her lines, because she has seen a dog she likes. Time and space do not exist for these people, and that naturally ruins my work completely.

By the end of this book my characters are no longer a tool for my expression, but I am a helpless instrument of their whims and absurd contretemps. As I think of this I turn to the end of this volume where I find myself saying:

"... every limb in me acted regardless of my will ..."

What better example of my helpless condition?

In short, my characters have taken seriously the saying that "truth is stranger than fiction" and I have failed in my attempts to convince them of the contrary.

And now I want to express my gratitude in particular to Dr. José de los Rios for his assiduous cooperation, timely advice, and for having so pertinently contributed with the manuscript of my friend Garcia, entitled *Students,* and I also want to thank my characters in general for their anarchic collaboration, seldom being disdainfully obedient to my will, often going off on their own track and doing things, I regret to admit, much better than I could have done them.

After this, and considering that the action of this book develops mainly in Spain, a land in which not the thought nor the word, but the action with a meaning—the gesture—has grown into a national specialty, I must beg the reader to expect nothing but that, which in this case, and due to the unreliable nature of the characters and myself, conveys no meaning at all but only empty situations.

As a contrast and a tacit reproach to this most impolite animation of the characters, the reader should exercise a certain amount of composure and under no circumstances show signs of the slightest surprise at whatever takes place. Sometimes the reader will find that an important character appears in a very inadequate dim light and in some cases he may entirely fade away. In other instances an apparently obscure character will assume a decided importance and almost conduct himself with all the resolution of a first-rate hero. Sometimes the threads of the book break suddenly and hang limp from my fingertips upon an abyss of futility; at other times they are joined together, strengthened and then bound about my subdued wrists into some sort of fatal and inevitable finality.

One must bear in mind that these people are creating their own life and standards, and are still novices at the game. In other words, the reader is expected to sit back and watch this procession of strange people and distorted phenomena without even a critical eye. To look for anything else, or to take seriously this bevy of irresponsible puppets and the inconsistency of the author, would not be advisable, as by doing so and imagining things that might lend themselves to misinterpretation, the reader would only disclose, beneath a more or less entertaining comedy of meaningless gestures, the vulgar aspects of a common tragedy.

New York, 1928.

Identity

IN WRITING THIS STORY, I AM FULFILLING A PROMISE TO MY POOR friend Fulano.

My friend Fulano was the least important of men and this was the great tragedy of his life. Fulano had come to this world with the undaunted purpose of being famous and he had failed completely, developing into the most obscure person. He had tried all possible plans of acquiring importance, popularity, public acknowledgment, etc., and the world with a grim determination persistently refused to acknowledge even his existence.

It seems that about Fulano's personality, if we are to grant him a personality, hung a cloud of inattention which withstood his almost heroic assaults to break through it.

Fulano made the utmost efforts to be noticed, and people constantly missed him.

I have seen Fulano shake hands during an introduction in a vehement way, stare violently and shake his face close to the other person's, literally yelling:

"*Tanto gusto en conocerle.*"

And the next moment, the other individual was talking to somebody else, completely oblivious of Fulano.

I have seen Fulano at another introduction remain seated and extend two fingers in the most supercilious manner. Nothing! All in vain. A second after the other person had absolutely forgotten his existence and was blankly looking through him.

On one occasion I introduced Fulano to a friend and had to repeat three times:

"Please meet my friend Fulano." In a normal voice.

"Please meet my friend Fulano." In a louder voice.

"Please meet my friend Fulano." At the top of my voice.

The friend looked around several times and at last he perceived Fulano almost on top of him, shaking him by the shoulders with murder in his eyes.

He opened his mouth and uttered in the most discouraging manner:

"Oh . . . how do you do?"

Poor Fulano's unimportance had arrived at the degree of making him almost invisible and inaudible. His name was unimportant, his face and figure were unimportant, his attire was unimportant and his whole life was unimportant. In fact, I don't know how I, myself, ever noticed him. True enough that he crushed my hand, dislocated my arm and kicked me on the shin when I met him.

Fulano had read all the pamphlets entitled: "Personal Magnetism," "Individuality and Success," etc. He had exhausted all the man-building literature, and in vain. One day he stood in the middle of La Puerta del Sol shouting:

"Fire . . . fire . . . !"

But no one seemed to hear him and at last he had to quit his post because a trolley car nearly ran him down.

Another day he threw a stone at a window of a well-known jewelry shop. At the noise of the broken glass, the owner came out. He looked at the window, and disregarding Fulano completely, muttered:

"Well, well, I wonder how that happened," and went back inside.

Not even beggars approached Fulano for alms.

All this would have been considered a blessing by a more practical person, but Fulano had no other purpose in his life except to be important, to attract attention, and these things made him only the more desperate.

Once I was at the Café de los Locos in Toledo. Bad writers were in the habit of coming to that café in quest of characters, and I came now and then among them. At that particular place one could find some very good secondhand bargains and also some fairly good, cheap, new material. As fashion has a great deal to do with market value, one could find at that place some characters who in their time had been glorious and served under famous geniuses, but who for some time had been out of a job, due to the change of literary trend toward other ideals.

I remember seeing there a poor and shabby lean fellow. He claimed to have served Cervantes. Well, the poor man could interest no author at the present moment. In that manner, there was a score of good characters who had been great in their day, but were now of no earthly use.

On this particular day I had been sitting for some time at the table chatting with a friend of mine, Dr. José de los Rios, and looking around at the different faces and types. Suddenly I heard three blows struck upon my table and a hand pulled me by the collar. At the same time a voice said loudly:

"Here I am."

I turned around and saw Fulano sitting by my side.

"Well, when did you get here?"

"About half an hour ago. I have been sitting right here and trying to get into your conversation."

I apologized, saying that I had been absorbed in the contemplation of characters I expected to use in this book. After that, with no little difficulty and by applying some violent methods, I succeeded in introducing him to Dr. de los Rios. Then I observed that Fulano looked more dejected than usual.

"What is the matter? You look sad, Fulano."

"What do you expect? I have come to realize that I shall never be important, no matter how hard I try. It is no use, the world will simply ignore me."

"It is very disagreeable," I admitted. "But there are a lot of other people in the same predicament. There are, for instance, a number of husbands, preachers, dictators and . . ."

"This is no time for secondhand witty remarks. What I am telling you is serious. I know that I will never be important as a human being, and

I have thought that perhaps I might gain fame and importance as a character."

"..."

"I don't care whether it is you or somebody else. You are my friend. You know I am willing, and perhaps you can make me a great character."

I bowed under the weight of the compliment.

"If you cannot use me, then pass me along to some other writer. If you could smuggle me somewhere in this book you say you are going to write, my gratitude would know no limits. I don't care what I do, provided I gain importance."

"And . . . what are your qualifications to be a character?"

"The deuce! My very lack of importance. I shall be rated as the most unimportant character in fiction. You know that every character has more or less of a striking personality, that extraordinary things happen to all characters. Don't tell me that you will be ever able to find a character as flat and little interesting as myself."

"Well . . . you can find a lot of that in present-day literature . . . I really . . ."

Dr. José de los Rios, who had remained silent during this conversation, turned on my friend and spoke:

"Señor Fulano, although I have known you for a very short time, I can see only one way of hoping to get you out of your present condition. Señor Fulano, you must commit suicide."

"What?"

"I don't mean actually kill yourself, but commit an official suicide."

"What do you mean?"

"Just what I said. This evening as soon as it gets dark, you walk over the bridge of Alcántara and leave your coat on the ground with all your personal identification, all your credentials, your money, bankbook, etc., and a note saying that you have thrown yourself to the Tajo. Then you go back to Madrid, having lost your official identity, and there we will try to make a character out of you."

Fulano looked at me questioningly. I said:

"I think that what Dr. de los Rios proposes is very logical."

6

Dr. de los Rios went on:

"You see? This apparent suicide will also serve as a little step toward notoriety. It is fortunate that this has taken place in this city. Toledo, the Tajo, and the bridge of Alcántara have historical background and that will lend color to your action."

There was gratitude in the eyes of Fulano and he thanked Dr. de los Rios warmly, and I promised to do everything in my power to help him after he had complied with his part of the bargain.

By this time it was quite late in the afternoon. Dr. de los Rios had to go on a professional visit, and he left wishing Fulano a very successful enterprise. We remained seated at the table, and as Fulano had to wait until dark and we had nothing to do, I decided to amuse him by pointing out the characters that were gathered at the café.

"Do you see that fat, bald-headed policeman? He is Don Benito."

The policeman was unsuccessfully endeavoring to light a cigar with matches that consistently went out. Then he noticed we were speaking of him and assumed a proud air.

"Now look at that table by the window. The waitress who is laughing now is Lunarito. They call her that because of a beauty spot which cannot be seen from here. The good-looking young man who is smoking a pipe and pinching her leg is Pepe Bejarano.

"Direct your attention toward that man whose collar is open. The one standing by the bar drinking . . . there now . . . the one that is pushing that woman away and insulting her. . . . He is El Cogote."

At this moment two nuns entered the café and went from table to table seeking alms for their convent. I pointed at one of them:

"Look at that nun. The one that is interfering now between El Cogote and the woman. She is quite attractive to be a nun. She would have made a good woman of the world. Do you notice how gaily she smiles and how white her teeth are? That is Sister Carmela."

The two nuns had now approached a distant table where two priests sat, and were talking to them.

"Look at that priest, the one with the best manners who is standing talking to Sister Carmela. That is Padre Inocencio. He is supposed to do a great deal of good around here."

The two nuns went out followed by Padre Inocencio, who opened the door for them and remained there a while watching them walk across the plaza.

"Behold the bartender. See his splendid apostolic beard and the boisterous way in which he is laughing with El Cogote. He is Don Laureano Baez, an old rogue and very amusing. The old woman behind him with the sad expression who is wiping the glasses is his wife, Doña Felisa.

"Now notice that man sitting at that table. The one with the white wig and the poetic expression, who seems so distracted and aloof. His name is Garcia."

The man was smelling a flower pinned to his lapel.

At that moment a little dog, who was nosing about the café, began to paw the man's leg. Garcia gave the dog a vicious kick, then he tossed a coin over to the bartender and departed.

"Look at that pale lady dressed in black sitting at that table with a gentleman. Notice how she is going to sleep. She is Doña Micaela Valverde."

Her escort got up silently, took his hat and left the café on tiptoes. Doña Micaela, who was now fast asleep, did not see him go.

For some time I had been noticing a man standing by a table where four men sat. He was showing them small objects which he took out of his pocket and which apparently he was trying to sell them. He turned around and then I recognized him. We greeted each other and he walked toward our table holding a small object in his hand.

I said to Fulano:

"This is Don Gil, an old dealer in junk, who peddles his stuff around the cafés."

Don Gil approached us. He leaned with a hand on the wall and in the other he showed us a little Chinese figure made of porcelain.

"Here is a real bargain," he said, tossing the porcelain figure on the palm of his hand. "It is a real old work of art made in China. What do you say?"

I looked at the figure which was delicately made. It represented a herculean warrior with drooping mustache and a ferocious expression.

8

He had a butterfly on his shoulder. The color of the face was not yellow but a darker color, more like bronze, and as the attire was not very representative, I suggested:

"Perhaps it is not Chinese but Indian."

Don Gil, who undoubtedly liked China better than India, looked slightly annoyed.

"No, it is Chinese," he said.

Then I could not help noticing that the hand that held the figure was quite dirty and inferred that its sister probably was in the same condition.

I said:

"Don Gil, be careful. Don Laureano is going to scold you for dirtying his walls."

Don Gil withdrew his hand, leaving a dirty mark that seemed unusually small upon the whitewashed wall, and continued to praise his merchandise:

"Yes, this is a real Chinese mandarin or warrior, I don't know which, and it is a real bargain. Perhaps your friend might be interested. . . ."

Fulano gave a jump and let out a yell. It was the first time that a stranger had noticed him of his own accord.

Poor Don Gil was so frightened that he dropped the porcelain figure, smashing it in a thousand pieces on the marble top of the table. I fancied I saw a furious look in the little porcelain head now detached from the body.

Don Gil wiped the pieces to the floor and went away, trampling over them with a chagrined expression.

"Well," I said when Don Gil had gone, "I suppose you have had enough characters for a day. It is quite dark now and you had better get ready for your suicide."

Fulano scribbled a note saying: *I have committed suicide by jumping into the Tajo,* and said:

"All my hopes depend on this." He got up and departed, promising to see me in Madrid.

Now I, as the author of this tale, can see all that Fulano did after he went away, although I am supposed to remain seated at the café table.

Fulano went to his room. He gathered all his documents and credentials and started on his fateful journey. As he walked down the stairs to the street, night had fallen, and each step he took was like dropping a century into the past, until he emerged in the midst of a hostile city which died in the Renaissance and yet lived the strangest, posthumous life. Toledo was in silence, but Toledo did not rest. As Fulano advanced hesitantly, he felt the restless and decrepit lines of buildings suddenly agitated by a wind of the past, the pavement seemed to rise, fall and revolt in its stony unevenness, like a stormy sea; he walked through streets so steep that he had to lean against the wall to keep from falling and he rushed through alleys that ran down from the top of the city like jumping torrents, to precipitate themselves down into the waters of the Tajo.

Toledo comes to life every night. It is a city of silence, but not a city of peace; at night it multiplies its interests, it becomes a city of horror, of fearful dreams of the past, of dreadful historical nightmares. At the turn of a street, this impression hit Fulano with such force that it nailed him to the spot, as if turned into one more stony specter. All the shadows of things gone came to meet him from out dark alleys, from out sad corners, to condense and take shape, to make the night blacker. He could imagine the figure of Don Pedro el Cruel, his knees rattling, trailing along the familiar alley to the house of the Jew who lent him money. He could sense the heavy atmosphere charged with the deadly breath of the Inquisition.

This silence, this feeling of being left alone to share a city with the dead, suddenly revealed an idea to Fulano. Toledo, as he hoped to be soon, was a myth, Toledo did not exist. It rose at night upon its historical and aesthetic signification, forsaken among this loneliness of sterile Castilla. And thus thinking, Fulano stumbled on like a frightened, forsaken shadow after its own body. The narrow, crooked, tortuous streets fled from him, denying his path, mocking, snarling, like snakes in a jungle of bizarre structures; he staggered from one surprise into another, carried by this immense and irresistibly suggestive strength. He passed houses that were horribly worn out where they joined the ground, their stones blent together, and doors that were never opened

10

and through whose ragged bottoms medieval cats sneaked in and out. He heard the waters of the Tajo calling and all this past splendor fading away in eternal response, all this past glory slipping down the hill, sinking into the Tajo below.

Fulano knew he had been swallowed by this maelstrom of the past, that he had sunk back centuries in history, and had already lost his identity of present existence. He was choking from this overwhelming feeling of condensed time, he was hopelessly lost in this darkness of thousands of superimposed past nights, in this labyrinth of streets that tossed him to and fro, threatening to drag him in their ominous stream and thrust him down into the Tajo, into oblivion.

His sense of direction utterly lost, Fulano let himself be ejected, cast out centrifugally, gravitationally by this semiconical city, now spinning in his dizzy mind, and he crossed one by one all the walls of Toledo, each one framing a period of history, like conquering phalanxes seen in perspective, each wall larger and lower, descending the hill, like steps, falling down into the Tajo.

And it was in this manner that the city of Toledo discarded this insignificant individual upon the bridge of Alcántara.

In the middle of the bridge, Fulano stripped himself of his coat and placed it on the ground, pinning the note on the outside.

Having done this and ascertained that no one saw him, he walked in his shirt sleeves toward the station.

Fulano did not see what happened after he left the bridge but I, of course, saw it, and if a writer had the privilege of interfering or preventing the incidents which he has the misfortune to witness, I would have prevented what took place, for the sake of my poor friend, Fulano. However, if a writer could do that, all stories would end happily and justice would prevail in all literature. As this would create a great monotony, such power has not been granted. Therefore, I had to stand by and see the happenings in a state of utter impotence and indignation.

A man of evil appearance walked along the bridge. By the moonlight he saw the coat on the ground and stooped and picked it up. He fumbled in the pockets and took out all the papers. He lighted a match and examined them rapidly. He then saw the note pinned to the coat and a devilish smile played over his face.

With haste he put all the papers back in the pockets, took off his own coat, pinned the note on it, and donned Fulano's coat.

In the train to Madrid, Fulano did not notice a man with a cap pulled down over his eyes and a coat that matched Fulano's trousers to perfection. Fulano sneezed furiously now and then, but his mind and heart were jumping with anticipation and happiness.

The next day a local paper of Toledo carried the following account:

Yesterday evening So-and-so who had escaped from prison and whom the authorities were prosecuting, committed suicide by jumping into the river Tajo from the bridge of Alcántara. This has been deduced from a note pinned to his coat which was found on the bridge. It seems that after the many crimes he had committed, remorse seized him at last and he decided to end his sinful existence. R.I.P.

One day, after returning to Madrid, I was walking through the street of Sevilla when I found myself seized by the shoulders and beheld a face pale with rage at two inches from my nose.

"Hello, Fulano! But what is the matter with you?"

"What is the matter with me, you ask?"

"Yes. How did the suicide trick work?" (Of course, I had entirely forgotten what I saw at the bridge.)

"How did it work . . .? How did it work . . .? Infernally!!"

"What do you mean, infernally? What happened, then?"

Fulano took two steps back and stood there looking at me:

"Do you see me here?"

"A bit blurred, but I still see you."

"Well, I do not exist."

"What?"

"I do not exist."

"You do not exist?"

"No."

"But how is that possible?"

"Since I have had any use of reason, I have entertained strong doubts about my existence. No, don't look at me as if I were going to enter into a metaphysical discussion. I am talking seriously now. Yes, I had always entertained strong doubts about my own existence, but since your idiotic suggestion about suicide those doubts have abandoned me completely. Now I am sure that I do not exist."

"But explain yourself." Fulano had already spent some of his initial steam and could speak more calmly.

"Well, someone is now here in Madrid, enjoying my personality, my name, my property, my home, my wife . . . everything that belonged to me. And he is enormously famous, mind you, one of the best known politicians and businessmen, and accumulating a tremendous fortune. And I am nothing, I am absolutely lost, looking for some loose identity in order to find myself. But every identity has its owner and I am nothing, nothing. I do not exist. . . ." Fulano broke down and put a handkerchief to his eyes.

"But do you mean to say that the people who knew you cannot tell the difference? Cannot realize that this other Fulano is an impostor?"

"How can they tell the difference if they never noticed me before? I was always so unimportant, so absolutely unimportant!"

For the first time I realized in all its magnitude the tragedy of this unimportant man's life.

Fulano produced a newspaper and pointed silently but eloquently at the big headlines which said something very flattering about Fulano.

"See what they say about him. What they should be saying about me. He has taken my name, my identity, and with it all the fame and importance that should have been mine."

"No, Fulano, do not deceive yourself. It is not the name that has made him precisely. You would have never attained that success if you had remained Fulano. The man must possess the personality which you lack and he has made the name famous. Really, in a way you should be grateful to him."

"Be grateful to him . . . ! That is what you say after you got me into this mess with your idiotic suggestion!"

"It was Dr. de los Rios and not I who made the suggestion."

"Just the same, you sided with him and you are just as responsible, and now you advise me to remain nothing, while he enjoys all my possessions and glory and fame, and all that the world can offer a man. I must sit back patiently, glad to be no one and thank him to boot! Do you realize the inconvenience of being alive and not existing?"

I had to admit the inconvenience of such a strange situation:

"Yes, something must be done about it."

"Of course, something must be done about it, and it is you who must do it, you who got me into it. . . . But, my Lord! How did it happen that this man took my place in the world?"

I felt that I must confess to Fulano, that the situation compelled me to betray an author's secret. After all, to lose one's identity must be the weirdest sensation in this world. Therefore, I related all that I had seen at the bridge and mentioned the account that had been published in the paper the day after the incident.

When I finished, Fulano was foaming at the mouth and ready to spring upon me, but he was firmly seized by a hand. It was Dr. José de los Rios himself.

Fulano struggled to free himself and yelled at me:

"So you mean to say that you stood by and didn't do anything to prevent it, to save me from this horrible tragedy?"

Dr. de los Rios tried to calm him. I lowered my head.

"Fulano, my friend. If I could have done anything, I would not have hesitated to do it, but it is not in my power to interfere with the destinies of men."

"And I am supposed to be satisfied with that answer, to remain an empty body without a place in society, a supernumerary in this world. . . . To hell with you writers who can place a fellow in a situation like this and then cannot get him out of it!"

I lowered my head further.

"Forgive me, Fulano, I will see what I can do for you. . . ."

"Well, go ahead and see. I suppose you cannot make things worse than you have. Nothing could be worse."

Dr. de los Rios, who had been too busy holding Fulano, spoke now

"Señor Fulano, I was the one who made the original suggestion about the suicide and I assume the whole responsibility."

"But I don't care who the devil is responsible. I am in trouble and want to be helped out of it."

"Very well, Señor Fulano, I admit that you are right in your demands, but I can only see one way out of it. There are no loose identities in this world which you can seize in order to regain your footing in life. There is only one superfluous identity as superfluous as yourself, and that identity is under the river Tajo. Yes, Señor Fulano, officially that identity is under that river and lately you must have realized the importance of official things. That soul upon the bed of the Tajo is craving for a body as much as you crave a soul. Go join it and end your mutual absurdity. After that I am sure that my friend will try to revive you in a story and to make a character out of you."

Again Fulano turned to me questioningly. I said:

"Yes, Fulano, I promise to do what Dr. de los Rios says."

Fulano gripped our hands firmly. Upon his features there was the determination born from despair.

"Good-by, Fulano."

"Good-by."

That night Fulano was again upon the bridge of Alcántara. He had come to look for an identity in the same place where he had gone to lose one. He looked down on the dark waters of the Tajo. Yes, there it was, his only salvation.

And once more he saw Toledo covering its hill like a petrified forest of centuries. It was absurd. With all useful justification of its existence gone, the city sat there like a dead emperor upon his wrecked throne, yet greater in his downfall than in his glory. There lay the corpse of a city draped upon a forgotten hill, history written in every deep furrow of its broken countenance, its limbs hanging down the banks to be buried under the waters of a relentless river.

Fulano looked down and then knew fate and greatness; he hesitated no more; with resolution he jumped.

And in order to fulfill my promise to that unfortunate and most unimportant of all men, I have written this story. Whether I have succeeded in making a character or even a symbol out of him, or whether he will enjoy this poor revival, I do not know. I have done my best.

A Character

I

THE STORY I INTEND TO WRITE IS A STORY WHICH I HAVE HAD IN MIND for some time. However, the rebellious qualities of my characters have prevented me from writing it. It seems that while I frame my characters and their actions in my mind, I have them quite well in hand, but it suffices to set a character on paper to lose control of him immediately. He goes off on his own track, evades me and does what he pleases with himself, leaving me absolutely helpless.

I have, moreover, been particularly averse to writing this story because I intend to use in it Gaston Bejarano, my principal character, who is especially rebellious and always wants to do things of his own accord. He is quite a bad influence among the crowd and on more than one occasion has completely demoralized the cast.

However, I am now at the house of my friend Don Laureano Baez. He is not at home and I am waiting for his arrival. Not having anything to amuse me in the meanwhile, I shall set aside all scruples and begin my story:

Gaston Bejarano was returning home one night, when he met a girl. . . .

The doorbell has rung. I believe it is my friend Don Laureano. If you will excuse me I shall proceed with my tale some other time.

Now that my author has set me on paper and given me a body and a start, I shall proceed with the story and tell it in my own words. Now that I am free from his attention I am able to do as I please. He thinks that by forgetting about me I shall cease to exist, but I love reality too much and I intend to continue to move and think even after my author has shifted his attention from me.

Well, he is quite right. I was returning home one night and was walking along upper Alcala Street by El Retiro. I don't remember the exact time, but I know that it was quite late and that it was raining.

I walked rather fast and began to overtake a group that walked in front of me. When I was nearer I noticed that two men were following at a short distance a woman, who in the dim light appeared to be young. I regulated my pace by theirs and watched.

The two men approached the girl (for by now I was sure it was a girl). There was a short exchange of words between them which I could not hear well, and the two men crossed the street and continued to walk parallel to her.

For reasons which are tedious to explain, I felt an urgent desire to make the acquaintance of the girl, but I wanted no witness to my actions. It was, after all, my first escape into reality and I felt a bit shy. Therefore I followed her at a respectable distance waiting for the moment when the two inopportune individuals should disappear.

But I am growing impatient of waiting and as the author is not present, I shall take the liberty of upsetting the laws of logic and simply eliminate these two men.

Immediately after their disappearance, I quickened my step and began to overtake the girl. It was now raining quite heavily and she walked swiftly alongside the iron fence of El Retiro without minding the puddles, turning her head now and then to look at me. With the night and rain her figure was blurred and there was something of a vision in it, beckoning and luring, and I was afraid.

I waved at her and she stopped.

It was strange. She stood at the end of her own shadow against the far diffused light of the corner lamp post and there was something ominous in that.

For a moment I doubted whether she stopped to face an enemy or to welcome a companion. I hesitated. Her shadow pointed the way to her and I walked over its dark lane.

"Where are you going at this time, in this weather?"

What she said was not as important as the way she said it. I do not think that I can describe it. I was so surprised by her voice. She was a sweet type with innocent eyes, but there was depravity in her mouth and her voice was coarse and low, her inflection cynical.

"I am going to the corner of Alcala and Velazquez, I must meet a man to get some money from him."

I don't remember saying anything at this moment. She went on:

"I am late now and he probably will not be there. I will go and look around the corner anyway."

We were two blocks from Velazquez Street now. We walked.

And mind you. It was raining all this time, but I did not seem to notice it. Everything had changed inside and outside of me. I felt no longer a character. I felt real, fearfully real, like any other human being who walks up Alcala Street on a rainy night and meets a real girl. I spoke, too, in a plain and ineloquent manner as if I truly were a human being:

"Who are those two men who spoke to you?"

"I don't know them. They just wanted to have a good time and I told them I was busy."

"Oh, are you busy?" I stopped. She also stopped.

"I told you I was going to meet a man at Velazquez." She smiled in a way that started us walking again.

"You seem rather young to be out at this time meeting a man to get money from him."

"Young? How old do you think I am?"

21

"Seventeen or eighteen, I suppose. . . ." I was sincere.

"You silly, only the other day I passed my twenty-third birthday."

She had no desire to appear young and for once I almost doubted her reality. I liked the way she said *silly.*

During all this, I noticed two things:

First: I was terribly aware of the fact that her voice was coarse and low and no one will ever imagine how I liked it.

Second: Our two shadows were shrinking and gaining on us and, as we passed the light they slipped under our feet and advanced ahead, blending into one, growing larger, immense.

Half a block from Velazquez Street:

"I think you had better go on and meet your friend. If he sees you arriving with someone he might get suspicious. I will wait for you here. If he is not there come back to me."

She agreed with such indifference that I felt that the rain, the world and I were about the same thing so far as she was concerned. For a moment I realized that in comparison with her strong reality, I had become once more a character and everything about was just the setting.

When I was alone I thought:

Why had I spoken to this girl? Was it because of the habits acquired as a character, which had left in me a strong tendency to speculate on girls who go out late at night? If she came back it was because she had not found the man. That is, she would come back without money. Now as the character I am and as you will discover by the things my author will tell you about me, I should not be interested in her, in such an eventuality. If she found the man, she would probably get the money. But in that case she would not come back. Undoubtedly she belonged, like me, to the profession. I thought of her coarse voice. But again; she was a real being and I was only a character. Had I stolen into her world of reality, or had she entered into my world of fancy? Perhaps we were only between these two worlds, and were walking together along the fascinating frontier. I knew one thing: that our destinies were bound together and that either she would have to drag me definitely into her realm or I take her into mine. Who would be the stronger: she as a real being or I as a character?

And of course she came back.

I grew effusive. I took her arm and talked, bending my face close to hers. I said many things but again I felt real and of course eloquence failed me. For once I regretted having stepped out of my character. As such I could always speak brilliantly and in a convincing way. My speech was fluent and well chosen. But now I was speaking in a flat manner like a vulgar man. I wanted to appeal to her imagination and arouse her interest, but instead I said that I specialized in girls who spoke in a coarse, low voice and went out late at night looking for men to give or pay them money. I asked her name, what she did and where she lived and then, to feel the ground, I said that I was broke. Was she beginning to prove the stronger, would I definitely be dragged into her world of reality?

Her name was Maria Luisa Baez, but they called her Lunarito. She lived far from there and did nothing. She had no money either. But everything she said seemed to lack life. It condensed in the mist and rain and fell to the wet ground. Indeed, she was reality.

Then came the realization of the rain. I felt her damp clothes. It was necessary to get out of it. However, the weather, the hour and the place did not seem to affect her in the least. But I was human for the first time and I was drenched. It was imperative to get better acquainted because there was also another latent desire in me. I suggested a doorway.

"All right," she said and we went in.

Until that moment I had been but a description and now I felt real. Beyond the door of that sordid hallway, beyond the clouded sky, I could sense the stars, life pushing me to her. I never thought that reality could be so intense and plastic, and when she looked at me, I kissed her.

What happened then is beyond me. It was so unexpected that I doubted if that reality was anything but a dream. Her dense cloak of indifference collapsed. She responded immensely. Indeed, she was a human being and human beings are sometimes wonderful. And then such a strong contrast, for what she said did not fall dead but flourished on her lips.

Yet what she said was in keeping with her style of talking. The word she said was *silly* and I drew it from her and it penetrated me, shaking the innermost fibers of the male. It passed from her tongue to mine, through our blended lips.

If there is such a thing as a long kiss, that kiss was long.

"Have you a cigarette?"

Again she was indifferent. We smoked in silence and then she said she was going.

I said:

"I want to see you again, I must be always with you. Give me your address."

"It is no use. You will never find it."

And even now I do not understand what kept me from insisting. I gave her my address and said:

"Will I see you again soon? Write to me, come to me, very soon."

"All right."

"Take good care of yourself. Your clothes are all wet. Take good care of yourself, you belong to me now."

"I will always belong to you."

"Good-by, Lunarito."

"Good-by."

When I arrived home I was thinking that this was the second woman I had loved without an interest. The other woman was there in my home, perhaps oblivious of the fact that for the first time I had really been untrue to her, that our future relations would be now more of a grotesque pantomime, intensifying our mutual absurdity.

And even so I felt that the tragedy of our life had somehow been robbed of its strength. Yes, that woman who awaited me, that woman who was my lover, was like me, nothing but a character. Had I not ceased to be a character? I entertained strong doubts as I entered my former house of unreality. Yes, that woman and I more than belonged to the world of puppets. Did I really belong? Had I sunk back into my world since I bade good-by to Lunarito?

But Carmen, my mistress, was awaiting me. How could I find anything in common with her after having had a test of reality? How could

I cross the abyss which separated us now, unless I trusted to sheer romanticism? And after my fleeting escape into the human world I had no taste for that.

Had I truly been unfaithful to her? She could not deem my fault so great with a being that belonged to another plane, to another world and different standards. An actor on the stage cannot feel jealousy because his stage lover steps out between the acts and falls in love with a spectator. But was I coming back to go on with the next act of our eternal comedy? And a mere puppet does not allow himself to step out and live and love like a human being between the acts. No, he must sink back into nonentity.

Carmen was sleeping that profound sleep I knew so well. I remembered that stupor into which a character falls when he is not called upon to act, when his strings have been released. But I had been perhaps walking in my sleep and my actions thus committed, no matter how transcendental to my future life, did not concern her.

I thought all this and even more, but when I entered the chamber where Carmen lay asleep, I felt remorse.

And this is the end. I have not heard from Lunarito since that night and now I think that everything was but a vision. All that happened that night tends to prove that. Her supreme indifference, the fact that she did not mind the rain, the swift manner in which she walked over the puddles. Yes, the whole thing did not exist. It was a hallucination, and perhaps that is why there was no man waiting for her at the corner of Velazquez Street, for there could be no human being waiting on such a night for something that does not exist. Undoubtedly it was a vision. For that which is reality for humans is a hallucination for a character. Characters have visions of true life—they dream reality and then they are lost.

And this is my predicament. Here I am: a character who has stepped past the edge of the paper and plunged into the abyss of reality, who now cannot go back to his own world. My comedy has expanded beyond the footlights, I have fallen in love with a woman in the audience. Can she be brought onto the stage, or shall we the puppets invade the house and mix with the humans in a general drama?

What can I do? To go back into my world when my main interest is in reality seems hardly possible. To enter reality which I scarcely know is a tremendous ordeal, because I have no real past. What can I do? I appeal to the author to destroy me completely or make me all over. To make a character out of Lunarito in order that she shall be within my reach. . . . But no, I want her real. It was reality that I loved in her. Then to give me a past and let me be human. But can an author give a past to a real being?

I appeal to the author to solve a problem which is beyond me.

II

This Gaston Bejarano, my character, is in quite a difficult situation. Of course, he is the only one to blame. I interrupted my story and he took advantage of my absence in order to develop it on his own hook, with the result that he has made a mess of it. The whole thing has not come to a proper ending; it has been dissolved rather than solved for lack of adequate interference.

However, what has happened to Gaston is a good lesson to my characters. Now he is coming in a submissive way to ask me to help him.

In order to solve, or at least explain, the problem of Gaston there are two fundamental propositions which I as the author must present:

First, I must explain how I, the author, met Gaston, the character, and second, how Gaston, the character, met a real person like Lunarito, which after all is not at all unusual, considering that I also met him. What is really almost extraordinary is for a character to take a real person so seriously, the general habit being for people to take characters with a seriousness that verges on the tragic (this book is an instance of that).

Then I might make a character out of Lunarito, but I don't want any more characters for the time being, they are too much trouble. Besides, Gaston himself has said that he wanted her to remain real and this is very significant.

It must be borne in mind that Gaston as a character is quite romantic at times, although he does not suspect it. Now, if a romantic human being had fallen in love with a vision, which is not likely to happen, according to romantic regulations he would want that vision to remain a vision, never to take shape, never to become plastic and human, because that would demolish his ideal. Well, a character is entirely the opposite of a real being, although it is sometimes our business to try to convince the reader to the contrary, and for him a vision is reality. That is why Gaston, as a character, wants Lunarito to remain real, because if she became fiction, she would enter and form part of the world to which he is used and his ideal would be destroyed. Therefore nothing will be done along that line and Lunarito will be left alone for the moment.

Strengthening the fictional side of Gaston, which is already beginning to weaken, remains to be done. He must be shoved back into his world of characters.

After that, if Gaston insists on becoming a real being in order to attain his ideal beyond the boundaries of his own world, I regret to admit that I shall not be able to help him. It is not in my power as a writer to create real beings, but only characters and that quite badly. Only his will to be, plus the mysterious and strange ways of life can help him. But I would not advise him to do that even if he were able. It would be assuming tremendous responsibilities, it would be a character who, because in a dream or perhaps a state of somnambulism, met a real person, became a human being and took upon himself the responsibility of conscious willful life, and all the unconscious actions of his past; who by becoming real lent all his actions a profound, serious meaning. All the things that once were nothing but play would then be real and truly affect his life and that of others. It would be a puppet who, by falling in love with a person in the audience, brought real life onto the stage, broke loose from all the threads which moved him and made a tragedy out of a comedy.

III

But now let me see how it happened that I met Gaston the character.

At the time I met him, he was generally known by the name El Cogote and that is the name I shall give to him for the time being.

I met El Cogote through Dr. José de los Rios, but before I met him I had already heard of this more or less notorious person.

El Cogote was known in Madrid as a prosperous *chulo*. Even more, he had graduated from that position into that one more respectable and profitable: an *empresario*. He owned one of the best amusement places in Madrid and was a rather influential personality in the gay world.

How El Cogote began and developed his career is a thing which I don't know very well. From the contradictory opinions and comments of people who pride themselves on being his intimate friends, or who even ran an account at his place, I have confusedly gathered that he began as a protégé of a well-known café singer called La Pelos.

I remember seeing and hearing La Pelos in a café quite some time ago. She was a pompous-looking female with furiously black eyes, a very hoarse voice that smelled of *chinchon* a league away and a pronounced growth of hair upon her upper lip.

Even from the faint memory I have of her, La Pelos struck me as a woman of tempestuous passions and it is not strange that she should fall for El Cogote, at that time a thick-lipped languid-eyed youth (according to a picture of him I had seen in *La Gaceta*). I have been told how their first meeting took place, although, as I have said, it is not to be considered authentic.

It seems that El Cogote (at that time he had not yet achieved this glorious name) was sitting alone at a table in the café where La Pelos sang. As she passed his table she bent over and said quite loudly:

"You need company, *chiquillo*. Are you willing to spend ten duros?"

And El Cogote had answered still louder:

"Certainly, have you got them?"

This answer made her laugh and won her. She sat by him and

encircled his neck in her fat arm.

At that moment a stout, middle-aged gentleman with a large diamond ring and a gold watch chain, approached the table slowly, ominously. He was toying with a knife of fair proportions.

He tilted his *cordobes* forward over his right eye and regarded El Cogote squarely:

"It seems that you are filling in your own certificate of defunction."

El Cogote swept the man with a sidelong glance. There was a cigarette hanging from his lips that shook beating time to his words as he said simply:

"I don't think so."

The two men looked at each other long and in silence. Then the gentleman with the diamond ring and the gold chain shook his shoulders, spat a wry smile and went away majestically. His bluff had been called, and incidentally, El Cogote had just introduced a new school.

After that day La Pelos belonged body and soul to El Cogote and for him she went to the dogs. According to the friend who told me the foregoing incident, El Cogote never cared for La Pelos and only used her as a good thing. She gave him an apartment, money, silk shirts, the most fashionable suits with short jackets and tight trousers, baggy at the bottom, and patent leather shoes with tan uppers. In her carriage she took him to all the *verbenas* and he always had at his disposal the best seats for every bullfight.

And even so he was always running after other women and treated La Pelos shamefully. She was a very jealous woman and their love affair was a stormy one. In many instances their fighting assumed such proportions and their behavior was so scandalous that the police had to interfere, but it is said that El Cogote had pull with the Prefect of Police and always got away without trouble.

However, his popularity had increased and with it his opportunities. He soon found more admirers and protectresses and his career progressed rapidly and brilliantly.

Then came a romantic incident in the life of El Cogote, which I have also gathered from various sources.

El Cogote had always been in love with a certain young lady in Madrid. A disgrace befell her family. Her father was accused of some crime and went to prison. Some people say that it was a frame-up. Others say that he was guilty. Just the same, the fact remains that he went to jail.

Some people in Spain take such disgraces entirely too seriously and often seek consolation in religion. However, whether that was the only reason, which does not seem likely, or whether there was some other motive, which the friend who told me suspects, Carmen—that was the young lady's name—was sent to a convent in North Spain to be a nun.

They say that there a priest from a nearby convent fell in love with her and later committed suicide. This, according to my friend, is a fictional touch added by people's imagination. But what he tells me as authentic is that El Cogote and Carmen, his sweetheart, could not console themselves for the separation imposed upon them by her family.

The result is that El Cogote visited the town where the convent was and one night the nun eloped with him. He took her back to Madrid with him as his mistress.

Apparently the reaction from her restricted past and the still more restricted environment of the convent, threw her to the other side of the balance. Under the demoralizing influence of her lover and a mad thirst for freedom, she led the most unbridled, licentious life. Soon after their arrival in Madrid, El Cogote, who during his trip to the North had accumulated a respectable amount of money from unknown sources, opened a luxurious amusement place in which the main attraction was the former nun.

News of the elopement from the convent and her romance with the priest ending in his suicide had spread through Madrid and soon assumed the proportions of a real novel. Therefore their clientele was large and select, including many high government and church officials which ensured a great degree of safety and success for the business.

This is what I know of El Cogote previous to the time of our meeting. Consequently, I was quite curious to know him personally and when my friend, Dr. José de los Rios, told me that he was his friend and patient, that he was going to see him and that I might accompany him, I accepted immediately.

On our way to the house of El Cogote, I inquired from Dr. de los Rios what he meant by his patient; whether El Cogote was sick.

"Yes," said Dr. de los Rios. "Very sick. It is an old malady with him, too. He has always neglected the treatment and instead does in excess everything he should not do."

Dr. de los Rios went on:

"You know? El Cogote is quite an extraordinary person. He will interest you. He is not at all a vulgar *chulo,* he seldom speaks like one when he is not in their company. You know? A strange thing just happened to him and has upset him in a terrible way . . . of course, his nerves are in bad shape and I think that his malady has already affected his brain. . . ."

I reminded Dr. de los Rios that he was not telling me what he had started out to say.

"Well, he tells me that the other night he was walking home. . . . Here in the same direction we are walking now. And that it was raining heavily. You know? I have told him time and again that in his condition he must avoid exposure, but he never wants to listen. . . ."

"Yes, but what happened to him?"

"Well, he met a girl. . . . He says that up to that moment, he had been convinced that no woman could interest him for herself aside from his mistress, but the moment he met this girl that conviction abandoned him completely. He says that in a moment he realized that the girl in question embodied all the ideals of his life, that he knew he would love her always and would not be able to live without her. . . . Well, I have never heard El Cogote express himself so sentimentally before."

"Yes, that is unusual in a man of his type, but I don't see anything so astonishing in his meeting a girl."

"But listen . . . the next morning he opened a newspaper and he saw a picture of the girl and an account saying that Maria Luisa Baez, known as Lunarito, the same name she had given him, had been murdered the afternoon before by a jealous suitor. Mind you, the afternoon before the night when he met her. . . . Of course, this has had a terrible effect upon him. Things like this are dangerous in the condition in which his mind is."

"But of course you don't believe that."

"Of course not. I don't believe in ghosts, but the whole thing is strange. I made inquiries and found out that the autopsy of her body took place at three o'clock of that afternoon. . . . But, by the way, didn't you see the account in the papers?"

"No, you know I don't read papers much."

"Just the same. I then told El Cogote that in his weak condition he might have gone to sleep for two days in succession and that he may have met the girl the night before the day she was murdered. I wanted to give him some explanation."

"That is more logical at any rate."

"Yes, but it is not true, because Carmen has told me so and she ought to know, and besides El Cogote has ascertained the dates from the things he did and people he met."

"But do you believe or don't you?"

"No, I don't."

And then Dr. de los Rios and I arrived at the house of El Cogote. As we ascended the stairs we heard a voice yelling.

"There he goes raving again," said Dr. de los Rios. "For two days he has been calling for Lunarito. He says that he cannot live without her, that he cannot take that vision from his mind."

A woman in a red kimono opened the door for us. She held a handkerchief in her hand and showed plainly that she had been crying.

"This is Carmen," Dr. de los Rios said to me.

A very old-looking woman with an apron, apparently a servant, advanced toward us and stopped in front of Dr. de los Rios. She looked at him blankly and almost recited:

"If poor Gil should lift his head . . . If poor Gil should lift his head."

Carmen pushed her away gently:

"Go back to your kitchen."

And the poor woman walked away obediently, always repeating:

"If poor Gil should lift his head . . . If poor Gil should lift his head."

We followed her with our eyes and I was aware of a respectful silence. Then Dr. de los Rios addressed Carmen:

"Do not take things so badly. I will see what I can do for him. Are you coming in with us?"

"Oh, no, I cannot bear to look at him. He has such an expression! Besides, he does not want to see me. . . . I am terribly afraid, Don José . . ." She closed the door behind us, submerging the small lobby in thick shadows. We were silent again and I heard her sobbing in the darkness.

Since Carmen had opened the door for us, I had been under the impression that I had lived this scene before. The presence of Dr. de los Rios, that sick man in the house, the old insane woman and this other woman who had shut the door in silence. Everything convinced me that I had formed part of the same circumstances some time before, and all that followed I knew and expected. It was the strangest sensation of advancing ahead of time.

I followed Dr. de los Rios through a short corridor and entered the bedroom.

El Cogote lay upon a bed, the covers thrown aside, the coat of his pajamas torn from the shoulder down. He was panting with fatigue from his recent attack.

Dr. de los Rios said:

"I have brought a friend to cheer you. How do you feel today?"

With an obscene word, El Cogote informed us that he was done for.

Dr. de los Rios motioned me to a chair and then sat on the edge of the bed and held the sick man's wrist. He produced a watch and remained still for a while.

"Aha," he finished. "And how did you sleep last night?"

"Very badly, Don José, worse than ever. I had a terrible nightmare."

"Well, tell us your nightmare," said Dr. de los Rios in a jesting manner. "My friend here can tell your past, your future and your fortune from a dream."

There came a slight flush into the face of El Cogote.

And then he told us his dream.[1]

---

[1] I must confess that when I heard the narrative of his dream by El Cogote, which I transcribe freely, I realized that Dr. de los Rios was right in saying that this man was an extraordinary person.

In his dream he found himself again at the house where he had lived with his family as a young man.

At the end of the corridor there was a room that had formed a kind of superstition in the family. No one liked it, they were all afraid of it.

On that particular day, he had tried in a joking manner to convince them of the absurdity of their fear. He told them that in order to do away with ghosts one had to do nothing but approach them. He told them that it would suffice to enter the room and the fear would leave them. He was then the only man in the house. His father had died and his younger brother was still a child.

El Cogote speaks:

"In my dream I was playing with my sister. Not the younger one but the other . . . you know, Don José?"

And Dr. de los Rios nodded.

"But in my dream my sister had the face of Lunarito, you understand me? Perhaps in my dream Lunarito was my sister. . . . Lunarito has been in all my dreams. I have not been able to get her away from my mind since that night."

In his dream he began to joke and play with her and then dragged her along the corridor and, in spite of the almost savage resistance she opposed, he took her laughing in his arms and precipitated her inside the room.

"No . . . ! No . . . !" she cried and the door closed, silencing her voice like a tombstone. Then he heard her no more. Undoubtedly, in her panic, she feared to arouse the horror of the room with her voice.

He did not give importance to the matter. He returned to the others, they spoke and no one gave another thought to the incident. Some time passed, they all sat at dinner and through one of those things which are inexplicable in dreams, no one missed her at the table. They had forgotten her. But there was a heavy atmosphere and all seemed worried. All hung their heads over the dishes and no one spoke. I don't think they even ate, and if one could see better when one dreams, he might have seen tears in their eyes.

After a while, something was heard rubbing a door. The sound was infinitely faint but they all heard it.

El Cogote speaks:

"Someone said, and I remember the very words:

" 'Perhaps it is some friend of the children who is shy and does not dare to ring the bell, but as they are afraid of the lonely corridor and the room at the end, they do not dare to open the door.' "

The corridor was illuminated by such a dim and sad light that they all understood and there was a long silence.

Then he was the one who spoke with words of forced gaiety, which sounded strident:

"If that is the important reason that prevents you from going, I will go." And he rose calmly and his steps resounded loudly. But when he opened the door he saw nothing but the empty stairway. At that moment, he remembered and walked to the end of the corridor and stood a moment before the door.

El Cogote speaks:

"I placed my hands upon the cold knob and as if someone had been pushing against it, the door flew open and a body brushed past me and leaned on the wall.

"It was she ... Don José ... It was she ... changed, like a corpse. Her hair was white. She did not even look at me."

Her frosted eyes were fixed in a vision of horror. They protruded out of their sockets, flying from the phantom which hypnotized her, which she bore within.

"You have killed me ... You have killed me ..." Such were her only words. Empty mechanical words, as if by a mental repetition she had exhausted all their meaning.

What he felt in that moment is impossible to explain. It was a brutal, tearing sorrow. In a moment he reconstructed all his life linked to hers. She was so good and sweet ... ! And he had done that horrible thing. ... All the well-known love he bore for her invaded him, it swept his whole being like a squall and he hated himself as no one has hated anyone in this world.

Then the scene changed. There was nothing but a corridor, long and enclosed, without another door, and there was that sinister dusky light so typical of dreams.

In a moment he was on his knees, caressing her, begging forgiveness. But she did not see him, her eyes were fixed in space and he felt between his arms, her poor body flagellated by panic, shaking in all its fibers in agonizing gasps.

He said:

"My sister . . . my poor sister . . ."

She said:

"You have killed me. . . . You have killed me. . . ."

And at the end of the corridor, the door was still open.

At the end of his narrative, El Cogote was obviously agitated. There was a glowing flush of exaltation in his face. I don't know what Dr. de los Rios felt or thought, but I know that the account of the dream impressed me strongly. In fact, I was so impressed that I don't remember clearly what took place afterwards. The memories of that last and extraordinary scene rush through my mind in disorder. But from that confusion, I retain the intense feeling of a profound realization of truth which dawned in my brain like a blast in a fog, a feeling that I was living a moment of ultrarealism, emanating from Dr. José de los Rios toward me.

I remember Dr. de los Rios looking into space with his deep clear eyes. Then I can hear, without seeing anything, the coarse voice of El Cogote:

"Lunarito, come to me. Even if you were murdered before I even met you. Even if I killed you again in my dream. Do not leave me. Come even if it is a miracle. . . . Come before I die!"

And then the door behind us opened slowly and I heard a voice say: "Here I am."

Dr. de los Rios did not move. I stood up and turned around.

In the doorway, with her red kimono, stood Lunarito, his mistress.

IV

And now we come to the second proposition: how El Cogote, or

Gaston, the character met Lunarito the real person.

Gaston thinks that he met Lunarito at the street of Alcala on a rainy night, but he is mistaken. Gaston met Lunarito at the house of my friend Don Laureano Baez and he imagined the rest.

It came about in this way:

One day I went to call upon Don Laureano Baez.

Incidentally, Don Laureano Baez was one of those extraordinary persons who happen in Spain now and then. His profession was begging and he lived rather luxuriously on the proceeds. Moreover, he had founded a school for beggary in which he and other teachers appointed by him taught all imaginable tricks for arousing human sympathy, from the art of declamation to that of contortion.

However, Don Laureano was not a common beggar. He was an artist in his profession and loved it. Even after success had piled upon him, he had refused to retire and at the time of these happenings he was still an active member of the begging classes, holding a central corner in the business district of Madrid. Yet this is not the point.

Don Laureano Baez lived with a girl who was everything to him. This girl was one-fourth daughter, one-fourth wife, one-fourth maid and one-fourth secretary to Don Laureano. Her name was Maria Luisa and she really meant a great deal to Señor Baez. He, a past master in the art of speculating on human weakness, had thoroughly educated her in the ways of life and she was a promising pupil.

Being a girl, Don Laureano had impressed upon her that her activities were not to be directed toward begging for alms, as she in her innocent admiration for him had tried to do; but rather toward trading for gifts.

Don Laureano had directed and concentrated her attention upon a tantalizing beauty spot which nature had dropped on a corner of her body. That beauty spot, which, by the way, had gained her the surname of Lunarito, could very well accomplish great deeds, Don Laureano had thought, with his profound wisdom, and he had even made out these rates:

For one peseta, the beauty spot could be shown.

For two pesetas, it could be touched.

And so on. It would be unnecessary to go through the whole list that Don Laureano Baez had planned. It will suffice to say that he had not left unrated a single possible use of that spot and that, in his list, Don Laureano displayed an amazing sense of values and a deep knowledge of human nature.

Don Laureano was right. The beauty spot soon contributed largely to the common capital. Lunarito became one thing more: Don Laureano's partner, and as such helped him in many of his businesses in and out of his official role of beggar, until one day Don Laureano did something which compelled the law to offer him a choice between death penalty and life imprisonment. Don Laureano, being quite old at the time, chose life imprisonment, and Lunarito was left alone to mourn and honor the memory of her idol and look for some other master.

The day I arrived at the house of Don Laureano Baez he was not at home and I decided to wait for him.

I chatted a while with Lunarito who was pottering around putting the house in order and then, not having anything better to do and not being able to find a single peseta in my pockets, I decided to begin a story I had had in my mind for a few days.

I sat at my friend's desk, took some paper and pencil, and began to write thus:

"Gaston Bejarano was returning home one night when he met a girl. . . ."

Lunarito, who had very bad manners, came near and looked over my shoulder. At that moment the doorbell rang; as I suspected it to be my friend, I rose and went to open the door.

It was Don Laureano, indeed, and when I reentered his study with him, I saw Lunarito by the desk, holding the piece of paper, with a dreamy expression in her eyes.

Don Laureano called out:

"Lunarito, did anything happen during my absence?"

Lunarito made no answer, she had not heard him. She was not there. At that moment she was living in the future, walking with Gaston Bejarano along upper Alcala Street on a rainy night.

The Beggar

IT IS LONG SINCE BEGGING TOOK ALARMING PROPORTIONS IN SPAIN. This situation is now definitely established upon a safe, sure basis, having taken deep root in the Spanish soil. It is now a broad, solid organization which grows steadily. Begging in Spain is, besides a respectable occupation, a profitable business and an enviable profession.

Much has been said about the corrupted ways of beggary in Spain, such a topic being one of the general themes of conversation and dispute which resound in all social classes except those composed of the cream of this type. Much has been said about the sincere ways of beggary in Spain, especially since the law forbade the exercise of this profession in its purest sense openly, that is, without the aid of some small merchandise as, for instance, pencils or shoestrings. I know not whether such a law still obtains.

During the days following the promulgation of this law, which applied to the beggar as well as the beggee, a certain individual by the name of Garcia was walking in no particular direction, carefully scrutinizing the face of every passerby with the intention of discovering some friend or acquaintance, no matter how remote, or even a faint family likeness to someone he knew, that he might accost the person in order to borrow some money to pay his room and board.

Garcia was not a beggar. He did not wear the uniform. In other words, he was well dressed. Garcia belonged to another profession which, although having many fundamental points in common with it, is not precisely begging. The profession to which Garcia belonged may appear at first sight more brilliant than begging, since in a single stroke and with a bit of good luck it can net as much as a whole week's earnings from hard, honest labor at straight begging, but under a closer examination it proves to be less profitable in the long run, and begging is a much better one in principle as the field is not so restricted.

Garcia belonged to a profession just as popular as that of begging and which counted on just as skillful performers. Garcia boasted of being one of the best exponents, but now he was disappointed and tired of it. It required too much subtlety and brain work, too much being on one's guard. Garcia was willing to give up. This fact, considering that Garcia was one of the high lights of his class, proves that it was not as sound as that of begging, as I never heard of a beggar willing to give up.

Yes, Garcia had decided to give up. As a matter of fact, a friend of his, a certain Don Gil Bejarano, had offered him a position in the office of the Prefect of Police, his brother-in-law, as a fingerprint expert. Fingerprints were Don Gil's mania and he had taught Garcia all he knew about them, perhaps more. Don Gil had offered Garcia the position provided Garcia were willing to let Don Gil have part of his pay, and Garcia had accepted. This was, of course, a secret pact of which Garcia expected to rid himself as soon as he could devise a plan to do so.

But, the position did not begin until next month and Garcia knew that he would not get his pay until the end of that month. Like most people of his profession and caliber, Garcia exercised a tremendous amount of delicacy concerning money that he might earn through such a conventional profession as the one he was about to embrace. When Don Gil made him the offer he did not want to show any hurry or eagerness for fear of losing the position; quite the contrary, he had acted nonchalant and carefully avoided asking to begin earlier. Garcia did not want Don Gil to suspect that he was pressed for money, lest Don Gil might make the terms worse.

The dialogue ran something like this:

Garcia—"Oh, any old time."

Don Gil—"Will next month do?"

Garcia—"Certainly, whenever you want; there is no hurry."

Don Gil—"All right, next month, then."

Garcia—"By the way, can you let me have five?"

And Don Gil had refused.

Garcia had decided to give up his profession in view of this last blow to it, and definitely accept what Don Gil offered. The thing had been arranged for next month and it would be six weeks before Garcia could get his pay. This was the reason why at the present moment he was looking for some victim upon whom to deliver the last stroke of the profession he was forsaking.

However, luck was not with Garcia and so far he had not discovered a single face offering the slightest excuse for an approach. Garcia was rather despondent. He had not eaten since the night before, he had in his pocket exactly a five centimes copper piece and a twenty-five pesetas gold piece. This latter, of course, did not count, for Garcia based upon it much of his social effect.

It is quite fashionable in Spain to have a sentimental story to display at café tables, or at a bench in El Prado, late at night, or at the moment of exchanging confidences. The sentimentalism about *The Mother* is a question that carries weight in Spain to exculpate an inexculpable individual. One often hears people say:

"He may be a crook or a criminal, but he loves his mother," and that settles it.

Well, Garcia, once in a time of buoyancy, decided to make an invest-ment. He bought a twenty-five pesetas gold piece which he always carried about with him, and whenever anyone remarked about it, he would say:

"Yes—" here an effective sigh—"my mother gave it to me on the day of my first communion"—a skeptical smile—"I shall always keep it with me. No matter how hard up I may have been at times, I never dreamed of changing it. Some people may think it silly, but what the devil! A mother is a mother, you know we only have one mother"—(a profound silence and a dreamy expression). Garcia had always considered it a great drawback to his profession not to be able to produce tears at will.

And now Garcia was facing the problem of having to change the twenty-five pesetas gold piece and dispense with his sentimental tale, since now he had a job and would probably need it no more.

It was while thus occupied that he was accosted in his turn by a beggar.

Garcia's first impulse was to laugh long and loud, but knowing that a gentleman should never take such liberties with a beggar, he repressed his desire. Besides, should he refuse, he feared his financial condition would be suspected. Even an unknown beggar's opinion counts under certain circumstances. Therefore, Garcia took the man into a doorway (for it was forbidden to give alms in public) and gave him the five centimes piece.

Immediately after, he went to a café across the street in order to change the twenty-five pesetas gold piece.

With a heroic and resolute gesture that was to put an end to his past life, Garcia slammed the coin on the counter:

"Change, please."

The man on the other side of the counter looked at the coin and at Garcia.

"Change for what?" He shouted loudly, brutally, cruelly. . . .

Garcia looked at the coin and then realized that he had given the beggar the gold piece.[1] Without regarding the other man's leer, Garcia picked up the coin and ran out of the café like a madman.

"Better use more sand on that *perro chico* next time!" shouted the man at his back.

In two leaps Garcia was back on the spot of the accident, but the beggar was gone. He inquired from other beggars the whereabouts of a man of such and such a description.

"He always closes at six," prompted a fellow without legs, from the floor. "He has this post during the day and I have it at night."

---

[1] Garcia had other plans for this story, but by substituting one coin for the other and creating an unexpected situation for him, I have him at my mercy. He has now no time to formulate a new plan of battle and I can make him do as I please and have the story follow along the lines I choose.

Another beggar told him the name and address, explaining how to get there, with his only hand.

"*Una limosnita por amor de Dios,*" said the fellow without legs.

"*Perdone, hermano,*" answered Garcia, rushing away. He did not want to part with his only coin.

Garcia walked in the direction he had been given, his heart sinking at every step. He felt surprised after a while at finding himself in a prosperous part of the town, by far more prosperous than the one in which he lived. He found the address in a modern building.

Before the doorman, Garcia hesitated, and if the doorman had not noticed him, Garcia would have turned on his heels.

However, the doorman had seen him and the doorman had asked: "*Que desea, caballero?*"

It was too late. Garcia inquired purely in a formal way, feeling quite sure of the answer:

"El Señor Don Laureano Baez?"

"*Principal derecha,*" was the laconic answer.

Garcia was nonplussed. He ascended two flights of stairs making different conjectures at each step. He rang the bell on the right-hand side door and before he had time to think what he could say if this Laureano Baez was not the Laureano Baez, a girl opened the door.

"El Señor Don Laureano Baez?"

"*Si, señor, pase usted.*"

Garcia advanced over the carpeted corridor feeling like an intruder, feeling his false position when he should annoy the respectable and important citizen Don Laureano Baez with his stupid inquiry.

"Will you please come into the dining room? He is having his dinner and will see you there."

Garcia saw an opening:

"Oh, I wouldn't think of interrupting him now. I will come back some other time. I did not know I was intruding. If I had only known..."

But the girl would not have him depart. He insisted, but she persisted in almost a diabolical manner, Garcia thought.

And then he was ushered into the dining room and there was his man.

Accustomed as Garcia was to remembering people's faces, he could not connect the two individuals for the first few seconds, so startling was the difference in appearance. He was facing a respectable and venerable gentleman of advanced age, dressed in quiet good taste, sitting at a copious dinner in which Garcia's quick eye discovered a bottle of excellent Rioja wine, another bottle of Ojen and part of a chicken roasted just so.

The least that can be said is that Garcia was flabbergasted. He felt sure that he was in the presence of no less a personage than the Minister of Finance.

And the man also recognized him and rose in the best style:

"Well, how are you? Sit down, sit down; won't you have a bite? A customer," he explained to the girl.

"Oh, yes?" said she with a solicitous air.

All this should have banished the last doubts in Garcia's mind but now he felt small, shrinking, like a poor man who has come to ask a favor or recommendation instead of a reimbursement. He did not know how to begin and fell on the chair which the girl pushed against the back of his legs. Since he gave the coin to that man sitting in front of him, every move he had taken had been forced. He felt in front of a superior character that for the past hour or so had been playing with him.[1] Following a confusion of ideas, very natural in his condition, Garcia attributed the results of mere coincidences to the powerful will which emanated from the strong personality into whose lair he had been trapped. The man was now regarding him without reserve, with a gay smile. But Garcia did not cough or swallow, he just began:

"I trust that you will not consider me impertinent if I . . ."

"Of course not!" exclaimed the beggar without waiting to hear what the impertinence might be, and he filled a small glass with Ojen and offered it to Garcia, and he also pushed toward him a golden cigarette case.

Garcia swallowed the Ojen and declined the cigarettes. After the

---

[1] That is what Garcia felt, but although he does not know it, I am the one who is forcing his actions. Since I had the inspiration of substituting the coins I have had him in my power and now can confidently leave him in the expert hands of the reliable veteran Don Laureano Baez.

past incidents he needed some restorative and something to give him courage to go on. The Ojen must have been powerful because Garcia hesitated no more and laid his soul bare:

"I am glad to see that you remember me. This afternoon I gave you a coin."

The beggar nodded his head in an affirmative way. Garcia poured some Ojen in the beggar's glass and then filled his own.

"I am sorry to have been compelled to take this step, but this afternoon I gave you a twenty-five pesetas gold piece by mistake."

The beggar raised his brows and opened his mouth, but Garcia did not let him speak.

"Of course, it is not the money. I could never dream of taking back what I give, even through an error." Garcia emptied his glass and the beggar imitated him, dissolving his action in a gesture which meant that he did not doubt his guest in the least.

"Excellent Ojen!" exclaimed Garcia.

"Ojen Morales," was the endorsing answer.

"As I was saying, it is not the money; of course, you know that. But that coin is not like all other coins. . . ."

The beggar rose:

"My dear man, you do not have to explain. An error, that is more than enough. We all make mistakes." He turned to the girl. "Lunarito, get me my begging suit." He addressed Garcia. "I have not emptied the pockets yet. Your coin must be there still. . . ."

Garcia also rose.

"Of course, it is not the money, Don Laureano,"—he felt friendly toward his host—"and I could not dream of taking it back without explaining to you. That coin means a lot to me."

"I do not doubt that," said the beggar uncompromisingly, and he filled Garcia's glass again and then his own.

Lunarito entered carrying with difficulty a bunch of rags of unsuspected weight, undoubtedly the begging suit, and laid it on the beggar's half-outstretched arms as an acolyte would lay a cassock on his priest's hands. The beggar cleared part of the table and emptied the pockets one by one.

47

Soon there was a pile of coins upon the table, a pile of such dimensions that it was difficult to understand how it could come from those rags which now hung limp.

Garcia spotted his coin among the abundant copper but he was too delicate to reach for it. He drank his third glass of Ojen instead, eyeing the coin surreptitiously.

The beggar also saw it.

"Aha, there you are, sir. As you see, we nearly always get copper." He handed the coin to Garcia. "I am sorry you had to come all the way here, although it is a pleasure to have you with us."

Such graciousness from his host overcame Garcia. He felt that the coin was decreasing in importance. He felt for the man in front of him the utmost admiration. He was conscious of remarkable changes inside of him, he was aware that there was a revolution going on in his brain and suddenly felt sentimental. He now considered that the most important find that day had not been that of his golden coin, but that of this great character whose existence he did not suspect in the world. The broad, frank figure of the beggar was standing before him, leaning on the table flooded with coins. Garcia had never seen so much money at once. He sank back into his chair and regarded the beggar with open mouth, shaking his head with a seraphic smile.

"Lunarito, take that money and throw it in the drawer."

"I would have never taken it back from you . . . but that coin . . ."

"We will speak of something else, if you please." The beggar sat down again.

Garcia turned the coin in his hands and insisted:

"No, I must tell you. . . . Yes, your generosity . . ." He felt eloquent, but somehow the thoughts seemed to escape his mind, they seemed to be thoughts that had a will and words of themselves, that threatened to pour out of his mouth, disregarding his critical ability which appeared to be weak. The beggar was looking at him with an indulgent smile. Garcia made an effort. He filled his glass and emptied it.

"Yes . . . my mother—" Garcia attempted a sigh. His throat closed and quenched it. . . . "My mother gave it to me on the day of my first communion . . ." he attempted the skeptical smile, but he knew that it was only a grimace—"I shall always keep it. . . ." He could not remember the speech he had so often delivered; there was something else that he wanted to say. "Some people think it silly . . . yes, there is only one mother, you know . . . there is only one mother. . . . Oh! There is only . . ." He felt choking, for once tears were coming to his aid. No, to spoil his acting, to give him away. He did not suspect himself capable of producing tears and now he wished. . . .

The beggar was watching him from the other side of the table with that profound, wise smile of his, and there was greatness in his countenance. Garcia felt small and mean before that man. He knew that the beggar could read through him, that he was laughing at him, at his efforts and failing attempts at hypocrisy, resenting having his intelligence offended so grossly. Garcia knew that he was a poor amateur before a great master in a profession greater than his, in a great profession; a man who had grown white hair playing on human sympathy and sentiments; a man who understood, with whom all this farce was unnecessary and useless.

And the beggar was watching him and smiling indulgently, almost like a father to a son, seeing through him, looking through him and recognizing beyond this miserable Garcia infinite other Garcias whom he had encountered in his long, intense life, disappointed at finding that people are always false and weak, that they lack the courage to be direct, that a man would lower himself to try and deceive a master for a small golden coin. And Garcia could no longer meet the smiling eyes of the beggar and felt the blood mounting to his cheeks; he felt ashamed, another new feeling he owed to this extraordinary man, and an overwhelming desire to be sincere, to confess to this understanding soul; he felt repentant and that tears were pushing their way out mightily. . . . And then Garcia burst out crying and reached across the table and pressed the beggar's hand.

"That story I told you about my mother giving me the coin is not true . . . it is not true. . . . I am just a dirty liar. . . . I have repaid your generosity with a lie. . . . My mother never gave me such a coin, I bought it myself." Garcia's expression was now quite comical, his staring eyes trying to assume an appealing look and the saliva dripping from the corner of his mouth. "My mother never gave it to me. I only said that for effect and everything I said was nothing but a lie . . . forgive me; you are a great man and can forgive, you understand. . . . I admire you, Don Laureano, I am proud to be your friend . . . I . . ."

The beggar assumed an expression as much like what he thought Garcia expected as possible. With his free hand he patted Garcia's hand:

"You need not explain, my boy." Garcia just loved this *boy.* "I told you that there was no necessity to explain. Of course, I understand, but don't worry. After all, it is all the same to me. Really, all this is none of my business. The coin is yours, you gave it to me by mistake . . . all this is . . .unnecessary. . . ." He filled his glass and drank it.

"I never would have taken it back from you . . . but I will be frank with you now. It is all I have. I am broke. I have not eaten since last night because, in my stupidity, I thought that the coin was more profitable in my pocket than in my stomach. As a matter of fact, I only had that coin and a five centimes piece, which I intended to give to you." Garcia produced the copper coin. "Here it is . . . have it, it was intended for you."

The beggar pushed back the coin.

"You need it more than I. I could not accept it after what you say."

"But it is your profession, this is a business question; you cannot refuse me that pleasure, at least let me feel . . ."

"Impossible, it would be a crime; it makes me realize how often men who need money more than we do, come to our aid and keep our business going. . . . Impossible, impossible, you keep it; it would be a crime."

The Ojen was taking effect on both men alike. The beggar felt now for this stranger before him a sympathy he had never given to anyone before. He felt friendly toward this young man who had come to him with the intention of deceit and then had broken down and cried in bitter sincerity before his obvious superiority. A tremendous affection for this honest youth who recognized his indubitable greatness; an infinite sorrow for this poor being who had not eaten since the night before, who had offered him alms at a moment in which it meant that he was giving his last negotiable piece of money away for charity. He was sorry for this man who, impelled by necessity, was now on the verge of changing a coin upon which he had based all the past transactions of his life. . . . And he also felt admiration for this young man who, on an empty stomach, showed enough character to admit his hypocrisy, to give himself away, because with an amazing intuition he had recognized in him a great man. And the tears rolled from the beggar's eyes.

"You say you have not eaten since last night?"

"Yes. . . . You see, I have accepted a position, but I do not begin working until next month. I have no money now and I did not want to change this coin because I depended on the sentimental tale attached to it for borrowing money from my friends. But your great example has enlightened me. I will change the coin now, I shall never borrow again. I have accepted a position and will work honestly for my money. . . . You have saved me . . . !"

"Yes, my friend, you are right; you must work honestly; follow my example; it is hard, I know it. I usually work from six in the morning until six in the evening, but there is a satisfaction in knowing that you have earned a modest living, that you owe nothing to anyone. . . ."

Both men looked at each other and again cried abundantly in silence. At last the beggar repeated stupidly:

"You say you have not eaten since last night?"

Garcia shook his head.

"Lunarito!" cried the beggar suddenly with a broken voice.

Lunarito appeared at the door and regarded both men with the utmost perplexity. They were holding each other's hands, their cheeks wet with tears.

"Lunarito, set another dish. This gentleman will do me the honor of dining with me. And bring another bottle of Ojen."

Lunarito brought the dish and the bottle and Garcia began to eat in silence. He felt terribly hungry; the Ojen had awakened his appetite, which had long since gone to sleep for lack of attention. The beggar watched him eat with a tender expression. Every time Garcia lifted his eyes from the dish, the beggar met them with a maternal smile and filled both glasses with Ojen. At last he cried again:

"Lunarito, Lunarito, bring another glass."

Lunarito appeared with a glass in her hand and a blank expression on her face. Garcia looked up from his dish. The beggar smiled:

"A toast, a toast. . . . At last the hour of acknowledgment between two social classes has arrived." He addressed Garcia, who staggered to his feet and filled the three glasses.

"To you, my friend, my brother . . . !" They all drank, Lunarito obediently.

Garcia felt a necessity to refer to politics as he always did when he heard the word *classes* mentioned:

"If the government only knew . . . !"

The beggar circled around the table and approached Garcia confidentially. Lunarito disappeared again.

"Never mind the government, my boy . . . you say that you are broke?" he whispered.

"What did you say?"

"That you have no money," the beggar explained.

"Oh, yes, I am broke, but now I am going to change this coin and that will carry me through. . . ."

"Change that coin? No, my boy, don't even think of such a thing. You said your father gave it to you on your birthday?"

"Yes, but as I have told you . . . I don't begin work until . . ."

"Don't worry about that, young man; after all, we only have one father. . . ."

Garcia made a doubting noise.

"Whether we have any certainty about the particular circumstances my boy, we only have one real father. . . . You must keep the coin." The beggar produced a wallet. "When do you say you begin work?"

"Next month . . . but . . ."

The beggar took a handful of bills and offered them to Garcia without counting them:

"Here, my boy, this will help you along, and if you need anything. . . .'

If there has ever been a grateful look in this world, it was the one which Garcia gave the beggar. He reeled on his feet, his mouth quivered and he fell, embracing his benefactor, covering his shoulder with fresh tears. He was sobbing aloud, crying words of thanks. At last he fell on his knees and insisted on kissing the beggar's hand.

Again Lunarito appeared in the door and her eyes registered the most comical surprise. Then Garcia rose and she saw both men reeling down the corridor, heard the door open and their voices:

"I would have never taken it from you. . . ."

"If you ever need anything come to me as if I were your father."

"You are the greatest man I have ever met."

"The hour of acknowledgment has arrived."

"If the government only knew . . . !"

"Never mind the government, my boy; after all, we only have one father."

And then Lunarito heard the door close.

Fingerprints

THE ORIGIN OF THE THEORY OF FINGERPRINTS HAS BEEN CLAIMED BY several countries. Spain is among these countries and the man responsible for the discovery was a certain draftsman, very skilled with the pen in all detail work, who is also responsible for one of the series of postage stamps bearing the image of the King.

The son of the Spanish precursor to the theory of fingerprints was very proud of his father. He was rather proud of being the son of such a great man. In short, he was proud of being Don Gil Bejarano y Roca, son of Don Esteban Bejarano y Ulloa, the Spanish discoverer of the theory of fingerprints.

It is not known whether Don Esteban Bejarano y Ulloa ever gauged or even suspected the important application of his discovery to criminology. His main object, it seems, was simply the identification of a given individual or the unmistakable differentiation among several individuals. But there are serious and strong reasons to deny that in his subconscious mind lay dormant the principle which wove a subtle thread of crime and disgrace, twining itself throughout the future generations of the Bejarano family, as some superstitious and jealous people have pointed out with a view to detriment.

The Bejarano family had been always rather obscure and unimportant. It belonged to the middle class, a term which in Spain has a far sadder meaning than anywhere else, because of the fatal, everlasting qualities of classes there. It is difficult for a name to rise in Spain, the money factor being until quite lately devoid of much social weight and marriage being one of the few reliable means of lifting a family.

It is, therefore, by no means surprising that Don Gil Bejarano should be so proud of his father, that for him fingerprints should mean more than for anybody else, that he considered this discovery as the basis of his social uplifting hopes. For Don Gil fingerprints were the thing that made his name stand a bit above the hateful average which he, as all those who belong to it, hated so much. For Don Gil the discovery of his father was the first stepping-stone to all his hopes, it was a priceless asset. Fingerprints were something that distinguished his name from the infinite other names as common as Bejarano, without which he would have been drowned in the sea of mediocrity. Gil Bejarano himself was a case in which fingerprints had proved their value to the utmost. On them he based his identity. Fingerprints were everything to Don Gil, he had based his whole existence on his father's discovery.

Don Gil loved fingerprints, he thought of nothing else; they were the main theme of his conversation. For ten years he had done everything in his power to have his father's monograph on the subject, which he always carried about with him, translated into every language. He had accosted a German fellow whom he discovered at the Prado Museum making a copy of a Velazquez, and proposed that he translate the monograph into German. The German was not very enthusiastic, but Don Gil was blind in everything concerning this subject and he had felt sure that a shrug of the shoulders was an eloquent way for a German to express the most ravishing enthusiasm. Don Gil had written number-less articles, proving in a conclusive manner that his father was the only genuine and real precursor of fingerprints, that all the others were fakes and impostors. Don Gil had shouted and pounded on café tables. As a true Spanish patriot who cared for nothing but his country, he had insulted Spain. He said that the Spanish people were careless and lazy, that they never boosted national glories and never asserted themselves before other nations. Don Gil was sure that if his father had been a Frenchman or an Englishman, the whole world would know that he was the great discoverer of fingerprints. Patriotism and fingerprint mania had blended in Don Gil, forming a most deplorable product. Most Spaniards of the older generation always attributed to patriotism most of their actions. And Don Gil pounded on the tables and shouted and insulted Spain. Fortunately, Spanish people are indifferent and café tables strong.

Don Gil had now been working for five years on a drive to compel everyone to have his fingerprints recorded in the office of the Prefect, at this time his brother-in-law. He insisted that it was a necessary measure and he himself headed the movement and had his own fingerprints recorded there. The Spanish public is reluctant to do anything that smacks of compulsion or community method. The people have a horror of all matters of the law, of anything having to do with the police. At that time fingerprints had already acquired a restricted sense and somber reputation of being related intimately to the criminal world. Anyone who should have his fingerprints recorded would already feel like a suspect, a potential criminal, and the result was that the only fingerprints in the office of the Prefect, aside from those of criminals, were those of Don Gil. This Don Gil considered an irrefutable proof of the fact that he was the only faithful citizen and only patriot in Spain, aside from the young King, whose fingerprints, by the way, were not recorded.

Don Gil had no end of discussions with his brother-in-law upon the subject, but with the perseverance which characterized him Don Gil ended by convincing the Prefect of the infallibility of fingerprints. When their last argument ended, the Prefect patted his brother-in-law on the back and said:

"If I had your tenacity very few criminals would escape me."

And Don Gil assumed that air of benevolence which he could always command when he had conquered a stubborn case.

"Benito, fingerprints are infallible." This was Don Gil speaking. "If a man were in China—" for Don Gil, as most Spaniards, China was the best example of remoteness—"and while he was there—not before or after—his fingerprints appeared on a given spot here in Madrid, he and no one else must have made those prints, and I would say to him: 'You are the author of those fingerprints.' "

The Prefect was struck with profound awe before this ominous statement. He lowered his head as a sign of admiring agreement. He felt the weight of his responsibility in the eventuality of such a case as the one of the man in China. How could he condemn a man in China for a crime that had been committed in Madrid? Don Benito shrank further.

Don Gil pressed him, possessed of savage cruelty against the man from China:

"I suppose you would hesitate in such a case. Well, let me tell you that there is no use hesitating about a verdict when you can base it on fingerprints. I would not hesitate, I would tell the man from China . . ."

Don Benito was already conquered. As a true Prefect, persistence and not reasoning had a way of conquering him. He felt that fingerprints were an enormous contribution, if not to justice, at least to those who administer it. He felt that fingerprints would in a case of doubt ease the conscience completely, relieve it of the burden of discrimination. Don Benito could shrink no further. His brother-in-law was bending over him, gesticulating like a fearful personification of divine justice, shouting in his face, pointing an accusing finger as if he saw in him the man from China. Don Benito could only murmur:

"I don't see in what capacity you would mingle in the affairs of that man from China."

But Don Gil knew that he had already won and utterly disregarded this last worthless objection, which, after all, had no bearing upon the matter.

"Benito, come over to the house Wednesday night; you know we always play cards Wednesday nights. Padre Inocencio will be there. You and he have something in common. You threaten faults with jail, he threatens them with hell." Don Gil laughed as his mind formed a series of comparisons which he considered both deep and satirical. "Besides, Felisa says that for a brother you come to see her very seldom."

"She knows as well as you how busy I am. Really, Gil, sometimes I don't leave the office until twelve and one o'clock at night. But tell her that I will do my best to be there Wednesday."

Don Gil thrust his hand in his pocket very slowly and Don Benito made a magnanimous gesture:

"Don't bother. I will pay the café."

This was a ritual which always took place when the Prefect and his brother-in-law went to a café together and Don Gil followed it up with another ritual:

"By the way, Benito . . ."

"How much do you need, Gil?"

"Twenty-five pesetas will do. You know it is a case . . ."

"Don't explain, please, Gil, such a trifle," and Don Benito took out his wallet and delivered the twenty-five pesetas as one who drops them into a bottomless well.

"Thanks, Benito; I will give them back to you on Wednesday."

"If you don't lose them at cards before I get there."

"Now, you know we only play with *garbanzos*."

They both laughed and departed.

On his way home Don Gil bought a newspaper. He looked through it quickly. Toward the back he found his article, the last of a series in which he proved the legitimacy of his father's discovery, its importance and infallibility. It was the last article. Now he was ready to collect them and publish them in book form, together with his father's monograph. He felt sure that Benito would lend him the money to pay the publishers. He had not talked and argued and convinced all that afternoon in vain. After all, this time the money would be for the cause. Benito had lent him money so many times for things that could not compare with this one! This time it was for the cause, for the great cause of his life. His father had never been recognized, but now it would be different. The name Bejarano would stand out. The Bejaranos would be an important family in Spain. He could not allow his father's memory to die out in obscurity. Spain had produced too many forgotten glories, too many unrecognized geniuses. He would not let his father go to join the Perals and Losadas in oblivion. Don Gil banked everything on the publication of his book entitled *Fingerprints* which, as he had often said, was a simple, short, snappy title that went home. If only his father had had his modern ideas he wouldn't have been so long

61

unrecognized. Don Gil was now sure that the Prefect would lend him the money. He caressed the twenty-five pesetas in his pocket. Yes, he had lent him this money without explanations; why should he not lend him money for the great cause, for a thing that would make him proud to have a sister married to a Bejarano? And Don Gil decided that he had already given too much thought to the matter and began to read the last article of his series, entitled: *Fingerprints, a sure antidote against all alibis.*

On Wednesday night Don Gil was at home. He lived with his wife, Felisa, and four children: two boys, Gaston and Pepe; and two girls, Mignon and Carmen. Now, Don Gil abhorred anything that sounded French. As a real patriot he used no reasoning for his dislike—he hated the French simply for being French. His wife, on the other hand, entertained a sincere admiration for the neighbors across the Pyrenees, but as a true woman she used no more reasoning for her preference. She simply loved the French for being French.

This disparity of opinions formed the basis of most of their arguments and had cast the few clouds which had speckled the otherwise limpid sky of their married life. When their first child was born they argued long about what name to use and at the end it was agreed that the children's names should be chosen alternatively by both (Madame Bejarano did not imitate the French in everything). Felisa, being the woman, had the first choice. The first child was a boy, then two girls were born and then another boy. In this way the foregoing names resulted. Felisa chose two names which sounded delightfully French to her. Don Gil picked out two regular Spanish names. But thereafter Don Gil always had a way of saying: "Felisa, your son Gaston or your daughter Mignon has done such and such a thing." And his wife never overlooked saying: "Gil, your daughter Carmen, or that son of yours Pepe, has done such and such a thing." And there was always a latent jealousy concerning the education of the children which luckily never overleapt the humorous limits until the time when Uncle Benito, who also disliked the French, offered to send Pepe (El Españolito, as they called him) to school in England. This created a serious family dispute which for years was always brought up whenever there was the slightest disagreement.

On Wednesday night Don Gil was at home. He was sitting at the *camilla* with two other guests, one of them a priest, Padre Inocencio, and Felisa. They were playing cards as Don Gil had anticipated. Now and then Don Gil stooped and lifting the cover of the *camilla*, stirred the brasero:

"These winters of Madrid are getting more and more treacherous."

"The hill of January, as they call this part of the year, is always bad. There is that breeze from the Guadarrama, which will not put out a candle but can kill a man."

"Those are only superstitions; nothing like the old newspaper under the shirt to defy all the breezes from all the Guadarramas."

Don Gil straightened up.

"There, now, when it comes to that, there is nothing like the classic Spanish cloak which, unfortunately, is becoming less and less popular in these days of foreign invasion. The Spanish cloak creates a warm atmosphere about the body that . . ."

"We have heard that a thousand times, Gil. Let's attend to the game," interrupted Felisa.

They played silently for a while. Padre Inocencio picked some winnings and mused absent-mindedly:

"Yes, these winters of Madrid are getting worse. . . ."

"Padre Inocencio, you are winning as usual."

"The Lord protects the innocent, my daughter."

"Who deals next?"

"My turn." The other man was gathering the cards and began to shuffle them.

"Have you read my last article in *La Gaceta?*"

"Yes, I did. It seems to me rather fatalistic, don't you think?"

(The voice of Carmen was heard from the next room smothered in manly laughter.)[1]

---

[1] The reader may disregard this interruption of two characters whom I had not intended for this story, but who are endeavoring to complicate matters on the stage by making noise in the wings.

"To me it seems that Gil is taking too much pains with that question. I have told him not to worry his mind, because he will never succeed. The Spanish public is too apathetic. If he only were in France..."

"But he is succeeding, Doña Felisa. Why, the records at your brother's office are now full, and a year ago there were not even three fingerprints recorded there."

"At least he could have got something out of it all, but he is too quixotic. He went and recommended that Garcia for the position of expert, which he might have kept for himself. You are too impractical, Gil."

Don Gil addressed Padre Inocencio as the most important person in the gathering:

"I could not very well accept that position although I know more about fingerprints than anybody else in Spain. People nowadays suspect graft everywhere, they would think that I was using the pull of Benito. It would not be good for Benito, after all. Garcia is a good fellow, he knows his job which is more than can be said about most Spaniards."

"What I regret," said Padre Inocencio, "is the turn things have taken. You have concentrated too much, Don Gil, you have concentrated entirely too much in the application of your father's discovery to criminology. It is a bad thing in my opinion to remind people constantly of the sins that are going on in this world." Padre Inocencio turned to the other man. "Even what you say, about the records having been full in one year, only tends to reveal the number of evildoers that exist. A sad realization, my children, a very sad realization."

"Of course, you believe that ignorance is bliss."

"I don't see that knowing does much good. After all, only the fingerprints are recorded, the authors of them are free. It seems to me, Don Gil, that the transcendence of your father's discovery was too broad to restrict it only to criminology."

"I know it, Padre Inocencio, I know it too well. But what happens? I conducted a drive not so long ago to have every citizen's fingerprints recorded. I did not want to associate my father's discovery entirely with criminology. After all, it was a sordid association for so great a discovery. But the thing had gained too much ground already in foreign countries and the association had been established. This public is not only apathetic, it is superstitious, you know that better than I, Padre Inocencio. The result of my efforts was that my finger-prints are the only ones on record belonging to an innocent person."

"Yes, the people think that just because they have their fingerprints taken they are going to get into trouble, they are going to be suspected. Why, I am sure that they feel potential criminals, they fear to become criminals just for having their fingerprints on record."

"Of course, they do. When I had mine taken, a friend told me that I was sure to get into trouble. The people are entirely too superstitious."

The other man, who had been shuffling the cards all along, began to deal.

"By the way, it seems that Benito is not coming after all. The poor man works too much. I have told him so many times."

"Well, he ought to, after you have filled his office with prints."

Carmen's voice was heard again:

"Papa, tell Gaston to leave me in peace."[1]

Don Gil was examining his cards.

"Felisa, tell that son of yours something, he is always annoying poor Carmencita. I think he needs a woman. He is old enough to go out and get himself something without having to pick on his younger sister."

Doña Felisa put down her cards.

"Of course, Carmencita is an angel. She is so innocent. . . ! You know that girl is too precocious and forward. Besides, they are probably playing and nothing else. You should not even make the remotest suggestion about certain things, but when it comes to Gaston you delight in casting the lowest suspicions on his character. I would have never thought of such a thing, but now that you suggest it so freely, I tell you that your dear Carmencita needs watching."

Padre Inocencio knitted his brows. He probably held a good hand

---

[1] For the second time these two characters are forcing themselves into this narrative against my orders. I had purposely placed them away in another room from that in which this scene is taking place, but since they cannot be seen, they are making themselves heard, and I am afraid we can no longer disregard them, as the other characters have already heard them and taken notice.

and was annoyed at the interruption in the game.

"Children, children, don't quarrel, let us . . ."

"No, Padre Inocencio, you yourself must have noticed how this man picks on that poor boy. The other day I wanted to get a tonic because the boy is a bit pale and thin and he immediately began to say that it was not tonics that he needed and went on speaking about bad habits. Why, the poor fellow is never free. You know that is too much, Padre Inocencio."

"Don't take it that way, Doña Felisa, you know all fathers take an interest in their children, let us . . ."

"That is not interest, Padre Inocencio; if it were, he would not be telling the boy to go in the streets and pick up women. I actually heard him tell Gaston that. He is literally casting the boy in the gutter. And anyway a father should never take such liberties with a son. Do you think, Padre Inocencio, that it is right for a father to tell a son to go and sin? Not to mention the diseases he may contract. Don't tell me that it is an interest, Padre Inocencio. Do you think it is right to give a young man that sort of advice?"

"I don't think it is necessary, but let us . . ."

"Of course, it is not right. But probably that is the kind of young man that Gil was in his day. But Gaston is a nice boy who prefers to think of his studies instead of chasing common women. Anyway the poor boy would not be so thin and pale if he had been given a chance like the little Pepe el Españolito instead of being cooped up in this house." All this had been spoken in a low voice. Doña Felisa was now addressing Don Gil with concentrated rage. "You should be ashamed of the filthy ideas that you cherish in your mind."

Gaston and Carmen were now silent in the other room; Don Gil had been stirring the brasero, facing his wife's attack with a bowed head and a tolerant smile. Now he leaned back in his chair.

"Padre Inocencio, I don't think it is wrong for a modern father to initiate a son in the ways of life. Sooner or later he will face life and it is better to put him wise to it in time. I am not casting the boy in the gutter, I am merely trying to show him so that when the moment arrives he will be able to walk in it without getting too muddy. As a matter of fact I have only spoken once openly to Gaston. I am not telling the boy to sin, what the devil! It is not a sin for a young man to be with a woman now and then. After all, we have all been young and you very well know, Padre Inocencio, that men have certain necessities that cannot be dispensed with. You know that if an instinct is repressed it may degenerate."

"I don't agree with you, Don Gil, I cannot agree with you on that point. Take for instance men of our profession. We repress our instincts and in the end we are no longer subject to those that you call necessities. You know our saying: Leave the flesh alone for a month and the flesh will leave you alone for three."

"And probably that is why so many of our amusement establishments have a back entrance and so many of the gentlemen of the frock are seen entering through that back door." Don Gil laughed and poked the priest in the ribs. "Of course that must be when the three months are over, since I don't see the necessity of using a back door when one enters a place to preach."

Padre Inocencio also laughed.

"There are always those who do not take their vows seriously, but let us play."

"Yes, let us proceed."

Peace had been reestablished and Don Gil turned to his wife and pulled her nose.

"This will be the last hand, Felisa, what about serving the chocolate; I don't think it is any use waiting for Benito, it is not likely that he will come so late."

Doña Felisa rose and left the men to finish the hand alone.

"You win, Padre Inocencio, I have had terrible luck tonight, not a single hand. You are too strong a player for us."

Suddenly the voice of Doña Felisa was heard in the other room shrill and broken, also the voices of Gaston and Carmen. Only snatches could be heard:

"My Lord, you two . . ."

"Don't be silly, mother, you are seeing things. . . ."

"This is the worst curse that can befall a family. . . . Carmen, you little *puta,* come here."

There was a silence. Don Gil inquired aloud:

"What is the matter?" He was disregarded.

The voice of Doña Felisa was heard again:

"Thank God, I arrived in time." Her voice sounded broken and damp as if wrapped in tears.

"But I tell you we were only playing . . ."

"In my own home, who could suspect such a . . ."

Don Gil started to rise, but Padre Inocencio held him down. Don Gil shouted again:

"Felisa, what is the matter?"

But there was no answer.

There was another silence, a longer silence. Don Gil stirred the brasero. Padre Inocencio was toying with the crucifix that hung on his breast, the other man began to look at the cards as if they were an object of the utmost curiosity. Steps were heard down the corridor and the front door was banged.

And then Doña Felisa entered carrying a tray with the chocolate. She was deathly pale and her eyes were very red.

"What happened, Felisa? What was all the noise about?"

"Nothing, Gil, the usual scold to the children." She addressed Padre Inocencio and the other man: "Now you behold home life in all its glory, a mother always after her children. They do not give me a moment's peace." She smiled, but as she laid the cups on the *camilla* her hands were trembling.

"But I heard the front door bang, Felisa. Who went out?"

Doña Felisa gave her husband a reproachful look for pressing the matter. Then she smiled again:

"Oh, that was Gaston. He went out to get something."

Padre Inocencio was tactful. He dipped a biscuit in his chocolate and exclaimed:

"Oh, the delightful *socunuco. . . ! Gaudemus.*"

They all began to dip their biscuits and no one said a word. The doorbell rang.

Don Gil made a motion but his wife got ahead of him. She walked down the corridor and after a little while her voice was heard:

"Why, Benito! We thought you were not coming, you are just in time for the chocolate."

When they entered the room she was saying:

"But of course you must have time for one cup."

The Prefect appeared concerned and nervous. They all greeted him and Don Gil rushed for another chair.

"Please don't bother, I tell you I cannot stay. I just came to get Gil. It is a matter of importance which requires my immediate attention. Gil, can you get your hat and coat and come with me right away?"

"Yes . . . certainly." Don Gil moved away to gather his coat and hat.

"What is it, Benito? I hope it is nothing bad."

"Of course not, Felisa. I am sorry to take Gil away from you and break up the gathering." The Prefect smiled politely at the audience.

Padre Inocencio and the other man made a noise like the one the acolyte makes during the Mass, which meant that it was perfectly all right, and from that noise the voice of Padre Inocencio rose like a litany:

"I think we had better go, too, it is getting quite late."

"Please don't, yet, Padre Inocencio, wait until Gil gets back. I am afraid to be left all alone. Besides, I want to speak to you."

"You are not alone, Doña Felisa," said the other man. "You have your children."

"Yes . . . but let Padre Inocencio stay a little longer."

Don Gil had his coat and hat on. He gulped down his chocolate:

"I am ready, Benito, let's go," and then added in a whisper: "Did you get the other partner?" Don Gil felt sure that his brother-in-law had a duel at hand.

Don Benito gave him a sad look and then said good night to Padre Inocencio and embraced his sister with exaggerated fondness. The other man also said good night and the three of them walked down the corridor. From the door Don Gil shouted back:

"Don't worry, Felisa, I shall be right back. Keep her good company, Padre Inocencio."

Downstairs the Prefect's carriage was waiting:

"If we were not in such a hurry, I would offer my carriage to take you home."

"Don't think of it, I live nearby."

When the other man departed, Don Gil inquired:

"What is it all about, Benito?"

"I will tell you when we get to my office."

"Are we going to your office?"

"Yes."

They rode through the streets of Madrid, sometimes the carriage bouncing noisily on the cobblestones and then with a sudden change gliding smoothly over the asphalt pavement. When they arrived there was a light in the office.

Don Benito closed the door and turned on Don Gil with an expression of amazement:

"Gil . . . Gil . . . were you mad? I never thought you capable of doing such a thing. . . . Gil . . . !"

"What are you talking about?"

"If you needed money, why didn't you come to me before doing . . . My Lord, I cannot believe my own eyes."

"But what is it, what is it, what are you—?"

"Your fingerprints, Gil, your fingerprints. . . . You know that they never lie. . . ."

"Of course, they never lie, but what about my fingerprints?"

"You know very well, Gil, at least don't pretend to me. . . . You know; Matias, the moneylender. Murdered . . . robbed . . . strangled . . . Gil . . . your fingerprints found on his neck, on his safe, everywhere. . . ."

"My fingerprints!"

"Yes, on his clothes, on the bed . . . everywhere . . ."

"Everywhere!"

"Yes, on the walls, on the mantel . . . even on the soles of a pair of shoes . . . everywhere . . ."

"My fingerprints . . . everywhere . . ." He repeated mechanically.

"Never were there so many fingerprints found from a single individual . . . plain, outstanding, clear, accusing . . . an inexorable rain of fingerprints pointing at you . . . Gil . . . !"

Don Gil looked at his brother-in-law sideways:

"What is the idea of bringing me all the way out here for a joke?

Come on, let us be serious, tell me what you brought me here for?"

"Gil, you know very well it is not a joke. . . . But, by God! We cannot be so apathetic before such a disaster. Here we are discussing it as if it were politics. I never suspected that I could receive news of such magnitude without collapsing . . . let me at least raise my voice . . . let me work myself into a paroxysm. . . . Men should not fail situations to such a degree. . . . Gil . . . Gil! . . . Why did you not come to me? . . . Why did you not think of Felisa and the children? . . . Of the blow that this means to my career? . . . Gil . . . Gil. . . ! Tell me that there is an error somewhere, tell me that you did not do it. . . . Give me your alibi, a strong alibi that will leave no way out. . . . Let us collapse. Tell me that fingerprints fail . . . that it is a false theory . . . say something!"

"Fingerprints never fail." Don Gil was beginning to feel dizzy, he was beginning to realize that it was serious and he questioned Don Benito, fearing his answer:

"How do you know that those were my fingerprints?"

"Garcia, the expert, the very man you recommended for his skill. He took the photographs, he went through the records looking at the fingerprints there without looking at the names on the top of the sheets. After he had recognized the prints he looked at the name and he wished he had never looked, for they were yours. . . . He was loyal to you, Gil. . . . At first he did not want to give you away, but then conscience got the best of him and he told me and left me to decide what to do. . . . What could I decide, Gil? When I took office I swore to myself never to falter in the performance of my duties. There has been too much underhand work and too many crooked police officers in Spain and I did not want to be one of them, and I swore to myself, I swore . . . But, by God! Gil, now I hesitate in the performance of those duties. . . . Tell me, Gil, I swore to myself, I swore . . ."

"You have done right, Benito." Don Gil was perfect. He had assumed an air of suicidal heroism which showed unsuspected histrionic prowess. "Your duty is to arrest me."

"But, Gil, surely you have a strong alibi, even after what you said the other day about the man from China . . ."

Don Gil had an alibi, of course, he had an alibi. . . . And strange to say

71

for a man with a good alibi, he knew in his conscience that he had not committed the crime, but the last article he had written swept his mind and the last stronghold of his human weakness.

The Prefect was watching him, he saw him thinking and all his hopes depended upon the conclusion of those thoughts. He was looking at Don Gil as if saying:

"Give the word and let us set the man from China free and not hold him responsible against all the laws of logic for a crime committed in Madrid. In such a case the theory needs correction, not the man."

But the eyes of Don Gil had assumed a cold sternness and in them the Prefect read:

"Fingerprints never lie."

And then Don Gil said aloud:

"Benito, let me see those photographs and my own fingerprints."

The Prefect rushed to his desk:

"Here you are. Here are the photographs and these are your fingerprints."

Don Gil sat in the Prefect's chair and laid both things in front of him under the green lamp. He picked up a magnifying glass from the desk and examined them closely, minutely, painstakingly, thoroughly. . . . He laid the glass down and looked at the Prefect with a blank expression. His eyes were focused on a point in the space just before Don Benito's nose:

"Garcia is right, these prints coincide. . . ." Don Gil looked again at the fingerprints and fancied that they were jumping, dancing in front of his eyes, mocking him. . . . He was now sure that they had left the photographs and sheet of paper and had grown tiny arms and legs. Now they got hold of each other's hands and the fingerprint dance went on. They were in space. Don Gil's eyes followed them, they were all over the room, running through the walls, through the carpet, through the ceiling, growing, multiplying, filling the air, always dancing, mocking him. . . . Don Gil wiped his brow and looked instinctively at his hands. The Prefect was watching him closely, curiously, Don Gil imagined pitifully, and looked into Don Benito's eyes and saw himself reflected in them, very small. He saw in those eyes a little man that was himself, dressed in a mandarin coat and pointing accusingly at him with a fan. . . . The vision faded, everything faded, he could not even see the Prefect clearly, everything was wrapped in a dense cloud of fingerprints that choked him. Don Gil was now absolutely aware of the rotation of the earth.

"Benito . . . have you an ink pad?" His voice was almost inaudible.

The Prefect opened a drawer and produced an ink pad. Don Gil pressed his fingertips on the ink pad and then on a clean sheet of paper. Again he took the magnifying glass and examined the fresh prints. His jaw dropped. . . . Up to that moment he had hoped, now hope had abandoned him. Don Gil stood up and burst out in a jerky convulsive laughter:

"Benito . . . I am the man from China, I am the man from China!"

The Prefect looked puzzled, only one side of his face registered a forced smile, but the flesh quivered over the cheekbone. He laid a hand on his brother-in-law's shoulder:

"Gil . . . Gil . . . I don't believe you have done it. I have thought it over and now I see how ridiculous it is. . . . Gil, think of Felisa, think of the children, think of what this is to my career. . . . Gil, there must be a thread missing somewhere in this net of fingerprints you have woven about yourself."

Don Gil had regained his composure. He thought of his wife and the children. He also thought of Don Benito and then he thought of his father and of the work to which he had dedicated his life, on which all his hopes of lifting his name were founded and which now threatened to sink him farther, away from mediocrity, yes, but into something worse. . . . Was it really worse than mediocrity? And then something immense seemed to burst inside of him and of a sudden came the audible, almost plastic, realization of all the happenings of that evening. Don Gil heard the muffled voices of his son and daughter in an adjoining room, wrapped in an exasperating, mocking laughter . . . and also the broken exclamations of his wife. With brutal clearness he counted the ominous steps of his son, on his way out of the house . . . and then he heard the bang of the door like a slap in his face, and saw his wife putting cups of chocolate on the *camilla* with trembling hands.

At that moment Don Gil knew that his wife, left behind ignorant of this other unexpected tragedy, was consulting with Padre Inocencio and making a resolution. He knew well what that resolution meant. His brain seemed to turn a somersault and his thoughts shifted from the past to the future.... He could see his daughter on her way to a convent.... And then his son who had left the house for good.... Again the present emerged before him with inexorable precision.... He had been wrecked, his home had been wrecked, he knew that he was lost. And the two tragedies of that night clashed in his brain and once more he heard the door banged and saw and heard no more.

Don Gil had thought more than the Prefect wanted and now he disengaged himself from Don Benito's hand and sank back into the chair.

Don Benito spoke again:

"Of course, Gil . . . you know it is impossible . . . tell me that fingerprints fail, that sometimes they lie. . . ."

"I am the man from China. . . . Fingerprints never lie."

When Don Gil was formally arrested an incident took place which I do not want to pass unnoticed because of all that Don Gil put into it of himself.

Don Gil had very small hands, exaggeratedly small for any man, and the handcuffs did not fit securely enough.

Don Gil said, and I repeat it because I am sure he would have wanted the whole world to hear it, Don Gil said:

"Officer, those handcuffs are too big for me. You had better get a rope or something."

But the officer, who was a typical officer, naturally failed in this crucial moment.

"You won't escape," he growled, "don't flatter yourself."

When Don Gil was being carried to jail, his head was shaking, perhaps only due to the jerking of the vehicle and he was repeating:

"I am the man from China. . . . Fingerprints never fail."

The Wallet

DURING THE 19— POLICE CONVENTION AT MADRID, A VERY unfortunate occurrence took place. Something went wrong with the lighting system of the city and the whole metropolis was left in complete darkness.

This happening, according to the French police representative, a most accomplished sleuth for anything detrimental to Spanish people, could only take place in the twentieth century, in Spain and in Madrid. It was a most deplorable thing, for it coincided with the undesirable immigration of a regular herd of international crooks who since the beginning of the World War had migrated into Spain and now cooperated with resident crooks in a most energetic manner.

As if all these people had been waiting for that rare opportunity, the moment the lights went out in Madrid, thieves, gunmen, holdup men, pickpockets, in short all the varieties of the outlaw family, sprang up in every corner as though by enchantment.

Now, the public of Madrid has a singular quality which, although praiseworthy, is appealing. This quality enables the populace of Madrid to get together at a given notice and perform great deeds, which in the end have no effect whatsoever. And one of the manifestations of this quality is to take ready advantage of anything that may lend itself to public amusement. The Madrileños are an exceedingly communicative people and they can cooperate to the fullest extent in prolonging and amplifying a metropolitan joke.

Therefore it is not surprising that when the lights went out in Madrid and crooks sprang up everywhere, people should think it a huge joke and want to join in. This, together with the seditious spirit prevalent in Spain which always renders an outlaw far more popular than any supporter of the law, gave such an impetus to this vogue of acquiring other people's property that many citizens who had been considered most respectable subjects yielded to the temptation and enlisted unofficially in the ranks of imported and domestic evildoers. The idea gained so many followers that in the end no one trusted even the most intimate members of his household, and it came to pass that during the Police Convention of 19—, Madrid had a criminal convention as well.

Of course, the police were bestowing all their efforts and time upon discussing matters of regulation, discipline and now and then how to improve the methods of hunting criminals. Needless to say, the public offered no more cooperation than the most bitter criticism and naturally, after each session, the police representatives and the police force itself had neither time nor energy actually to put a check to the outrages that were going on under their very noses.

Therefore all crooks felt safer and freer to perform their duty in Madrid, where the cream of the police were gathered, than anywhere else. This state of things, and the fact that lights were out and one could not see one's own hand at night, created too good an opportunity to waste.

I will not mention my personal actions during that week of darkness, but it is rumored that aside from many lost virginities and other unimportant things, some of the magnates (and this is an important point) who were invited to the convention, felt inclined to a bit of instructive amusement after the boring daily sessions. They decided to observe the situation closely, and indulged in an occasional holdup, just to see how it was done.

This is the only explanation of the almost unbelievable fact that during the 19— Police Convention there were more crooks in Madrid than there had been citizens up to that date, that a single victim was held up by more than ten persons at one time, that crooks held up each other and then issued a manifesto protesting because honest people were spoiling their trade, that sometimes a piece of goods would pass from hand to hand until it came as if by magic into the possession of its original owner, and that not a single arrest took place during the week. And this will prove the suppressed emotions and hidden wishes to which a public will give way, under exceptional circumstances and competent guidance.

After this preamble, which the reader may skip without fear of incurring my anger, and which has covered the first half of that week of darkness, remembered by every Madrileño with obvious amusement and subtle regret, on dark Thursday of that memorable week to be exact, Don Benito Calinez, the Prefect of Police, was sunk in a chair at the Casino de Madrid. He was a short, fat man, with a short gray beard and a short military mustache. The top of his head was absolutely bald, but in his particular case not shiny.

He sat with his legs apart, his abdomen being in the way, and his hands hung lifelessly over the arms of the chair, bringing his elbows and arms in exact level with the bald part of his head. The stiff bosom of his shirt stood out, pushing his beard upwards, giving him the appearance of a dove in heat, an appearance which contrasted with his dejected expression.

Facing Don Benito, in another chair equally comfortable but more in proportion to its occupant, was another person quite different in appearance. It was a young man, tall (one might judge this from the length of his legs which were stretched in front of him), with abundant hair on his head and a clean-shaven face. There was something in his general demeanor that bore the unmistakable seal of the foreigner (that is, from the viewpoint of a Spaniard). Perhaps it was his shaven face, or his extraordinarily fair complexion; perhaps it was only the pipe he was smoking, a thing which at that time, in Spain, was the privilege of a foreigner, or of a person who desired to be considered a foreigner—hundred percent Spaniards smoked a pipe only when they traveled in a ship, that is, away from Spain.

This young man and Don Benito were seemingly absorbed in the contemplation of a candle that burned between them (the lights were out in the Casino also). Neither of them spoke, the silence in the room where they sat was interrupted only by the distant sound of voices in other rooms and now and then by the voice of a croupier in the gambling hall calling out:

"Hagan juego, señores . . . no va mas."

After a few moments, the young man reached for the candle to relight his pipe but neither he nor the Prefect spoke a single word or made another move.

As I cannot describe any conversation or action, I shall endeavor to set down some thoughts, a bad habit which writers have of trying to convince the readers that they can steal into their characters' minds. However, I may be exonerated, since my characters fail me in a persistent way and refuse to talk or even move and I cannot very well leave a blank space.

Candlelight for almost a whole week was getting on Don Benito's nerves. He felt an utter wreck as he had been a central figure and the bull's eye of criticism for the last few days. He was enjoying one of those splitting headaches that threaten to become chronic. That shimmering flame that hypnotized him was as torturing as a string of needles boring through his eyes. As a matter of fact the Prefect had always abhorred candlelight and he was only able to tolerate it in *La Danza de la Pulga.*[1]

When the young man picked up the candle, Don Benito was about to tell him to blow it out, but then he cast a suspicious look about him, which included the young man, and he gave up the idea. His nerves were on edge after the happenings of the past few days.

The Prefect had had a terrible day. Again I will exercise the privilege of stealing into a character's mind.

Don Benito thought:

The night before, there had been robberies in number comparable

---

[1] The Dance of the Flea, a depraved performance usually given in second-rate theaters and *cafés cantantes,* in which a lady appears in a transparent nightgown with a candle in her hand and proceeds to look for an insidious flea which hides most cleverly, until it is found where every intelligent flea would hide.

only to astronomical figures.

The next day, several people had been found naked, tied to the trees in front of the botanical gardens. Why that spot had been chosen was a thing that puzzled the Prefect beyond description.

That morning his desk had been flooded with an endless stream of letters.

Don Benito remembered:

Letters of complaint.

Insulting letters.

Letters of reproach.

Letters in which several people accused each other and cast suspicion on the rest of the population.

Letters of mockery.

Letters saying that the police of Madrid were a bunch of good-for-nothings and grafters, a bunch of *mandrias*.

Letters calling him a jackass point-blank.

Letters insinuating all the things which open accusations had neglected to mention.

All of them anonymous letters, except one signed with a woman's name and very heavily scented, the contents of which might pass in Spanish, but in English would never do.

And Don Benito had resented this letter more than anything else.

After all, was he to blame because the lights were out? Could any other Prefect have handled better this public of Madrid that took to a new vogue, like a child to a new toy? Was the public offering any cooperation whatever? No, electricity was not his business. Any Prefect who was not a sound Madrileño would have gone crazy with such a people. The public was hindering his actions as heroically as possible. Everything was against him, he could not possibly place the whole population under arrest. He could not put a single person under arrest without being considered unjust.

It seemed that the whole city had conspired to mock him, to make him a laughingstock just at the moment when the foreign police representatives were there to witness his ridicule. He, the omnipotent Prefect of Police! Was the public beginning to doubt his omnipotence?

Had by this time the doubt vanished? That perfumed letter had shaken the last stronghold of his self-confidence. Was he himself beginning to think he was impotent? But then, the incorrigible Spanish tendency to puns graced his subconscious mind and he smiled thinking of his Don Juanesque escapades and rejected the idea.

The thoughts of the Prefect passed from the morning to that afternoon over a lunch which he had not been able to digest.

The meeting of the convention had been more annoying than ever. When he had opened the meeting, the foreign representatives had chuckled and he had overheard remarks conveying that a prefect under whose nose so many robberies were taking place should be hiding under his bed instead of making speeches at a Police Convention. If he only had the courage to tell those faces in front of him a few things, all the beds of the Hotel Palace, where the convention was stopping, would be hiding the ominous personalities of foreign representatives. After this, of course, eloquence had failed him and his speech had fallen flat.

And on top of everything, his nephew, who was now sitting in front of him, had unexpectedly appeared out of this darkness. He had arrived that week from England where he had been expelled from college for God knows what, and had even had the impudence to spend two weeks in Paris, on his way to Spain, in order to celebrate his expulsion and unexpected vacation.

All this the Prefect thought, and having thought, he said something which at first might seem not to follow the trend of his mind, but which would show to any elemental observer an intimate association of ideas and feelings.

Don Benito bounced on his seat and shouted furiously at his nephew:

"Pepe, you are a *sinverguenza.*"

This remark, after such a long silence, seemingly out of a dark sky, may not surprise the reader who has followed the Prefect's thoughts, but one must remember that Pepe was not aware of what had been going on in his uncle's mind and therefore it surprised him prodigiously. It even sounded rather comical and he pulled at his pipe more rapidly. After all, to be insulted by an uncle who has paid for one's uneducation and still offers the possibility of a generous allowance is not so bad. But as I was saying or rather the Prefect:

"Pepe, you are a *sinverguenza.* I suppose it runs in the family, I mean, your father's side. He was a dreamer and a secondhand Quixote, with the result that I always had to come to his financial aid. Some people still think that this is being superior, but I call it plain *sinverguenza.*"

At this moment, and at the Casino de Madrid (the place is as important as the moment in these cases), any regular Spaniard would have stood up (to stand up was necessary in order to reach across the table) and slapped the plumpish face of the Prefect. According to slapping regulations in Spain as applied to this case, one slaps the face:

First: If it is that of a stranger, in which case a duel usually follows.

Second: When, although a relative, he is not as close to one as the relative he criticizes, in which case a fight always follows.

But Pepe had spent several years in England, and many of his Spanish characteristics had been removed. Therefore let us not blame him for his diplomatic silence.

"Yes," the Prefect went on. "Since your father died and left my poor sister penniless, I have had to take care of you and your brother Gaston, who was also too proud to work. I tell you it runs in the family. When Gaston returned from that trip of his to Paris he had undergone a decided change. It seems that that city brought out his true colors. He began to say that the allowance I had assigned him of fifty duros a month was not enough to keep a gentleman, that since he had traveled he had learned more about life and acquired good taste and that he had decided to live in the way his name entitled him to live. All this on my money, mind you, on my money! You don't know all the things that have happened since you went away, things of which I don't even want to speak. And now here you come, expelled from college, having wasted my money in a deplorable manner. Is that the way to repay me for all I have done for you?" The Prefect was perfectly aware that his speech lacked energy, he did not know to what to attribute this.

"But, uncle, I have already explained..."

"Yes, yes, I know. When I read your letter, it seemed as if your father had written it. The object of an injustice! Of course, Don Quixote! that's all. The same stuff as your father." Don Benito was finding himself again. "Trying to make the whole world believe that all your blunders are but the result of your generous ideals and exaggerated sense of honor. . . . Lack of shame! That is what I call it. Look at your brother. What is he now? A common professional pimp, yes, a pimp and one of the worst or the best whichever way you take it."

The pipe dropped from Pepe's mouth, because just for a moment the foreign qualities which supported it had yielded to surprise and his face stood there naked, unmasked, pipeless, suddenly bewildered and unmistakably Spanish:

"What did you say? Gaston a professional pimp?"

The Prefect felt satisfied. His last words had gone home. The effect he had anticipated was produced and now they were both living up to the situation. Since the conversation had begun, Don Benito had felt that they both were utterly uninterested in any words, that they sounded void. He felt, and was sure his nephew felt also, that the darkness of the city which penetrated the Casino hung over everything like a lifeless thing robbing words of their light. He felt that emotion was lacking, that far from what one would suppose, it could not be aroused by this flickering candlelight, surrounded by circumstances that were more mysterious and consequently more emotional.

Pepe, on the other hand, felt something else besides. Having been so long away from his country, he had subconsciously absorbed the foreign belief that Spain is a backward country and that when one crossed the Pyrenees southward one entered eternal night. Naturally when he arrived at Madrid in this general darkness this subconscious belief found a strong echo in his senses. He felt like one who is dreaming (this, of course, is a feeling shared by most Spaniards who return to Spain after a long absence). Although the existence of his brother, whom he had not seen since he was a boy, was to him something mythical, the startling revelation on the whole had shaken him. The pipe had fallen from his mouth. The last chip of his foreign veneer had dropped from him, the only thing that remained to make him sti feel an outsider and spectator, witnessing the phenomena of an extraordinary land without present reality, had abandoned him and his race had come out. He felt again at home. Without the pipe he had been able to register surprise and even exclaim rather convincingly:

"What did you say? Gaston a professional pimp?"

And the Prefect had been satisfied. He knew now that both of them were feeling a common emotion. He felt confidential and friendly toward the young man. His resentment against his nephew was rapidly wearing off. Both of them were victims of the same family disaster. They were both witnessing a great common catastrophe. His nephew had not failed him. (Don Benito felt that night a tremendous necessity for sympathy and moral and emotional support.) The Prefect always hated people to fail in situations. But his nephew had not failed him, his nephew had exclaimed:

"What did you say? Gaston a professional pimp?"

"Of course, you don't know it, because I thought it would be better not to write to you about that. There are some other things in connection with him that I will not even tell you now. I would rather let you find them out yourself. But imagine! The nephew of the Prefect of Police, a *chulo,* a Bejarano and Calinez, mind you, a man who carries my name, a professional *chulo!* Because let us agree that quixotic as your father was, he would have never stooped so low, even if he served a term in La Carcel Modelo."

"You know what he did."

"Yes, we all know that story. Felisa, your poor mother, always said that it was another of his heroic deeds for a great cause. But do you know what I have always thought of the whole affair?"

"What?"

"That fingerprints never lie."

"That is another story. Now tell me about Gaston. You say he is a . . ."

"Certainly, he has been one for some time. They call him El Cogote because he never wears a necktie and always shows his neck. It started because, when he asked me to increase his allowance, I refused, considering that fifty duros is more than enough, especially when one does not have to work for it. Then he began to contract debts which I had to meet, until I got tired. One day we met here. He sat just where you are and we quarreled."

"Well, well . . ."

"I cut him off completely. Then I learned that he was in misery, but always too proud to work . . . but not too proud to ask his uncle for money or to insert, as he did, an advertisement on the front page of *El Heraldo,* appealing to his wealthy and numerous acquaintances, an advertisement that stood in the center of that front page like a spot of shame on the family, saying that a Bejarano y Calinez could not be left to die from starvation. He thought that out of pride, if nothing else, I would come to his aid."

"And what about the rest of the family?"

"Well, you know already that your sister Mignon died from tuberculosis, and as to your mother and your sister Carmen . . . Well, you had better ask Gaston . . . I cannot go into certain things. Your brother is a gem. In my business I have come across him already. He was arrested twice here in Madrid and I, his uncle, had to handle the case. The first time because of an obscene scandal. A woman who was supporting him, a woman whom they call La Pelos, because she has a mustache like a *Guardian Civil,* knifed another girl called Lunarito, who has a beauty spot in a certain part and will show it to anyone for one peseta. La Pelos said that she knifed the other woman because she found her in the apartment she had given El Cogote, undoubtedly showing him her beauty spot without charging the customary peseta. She said that she would stand for no cheap *puta* placing horns on her and all that kind of thing. The whole case nauseated me and I let Gaston go free, although he did not promise to reform."

The Prefect went on speaking about the other time when Gaston had been brought to him on a charge of grand larceny, but Pepe was not listening to him. The first incident was the most typically Spanish and had arrested his attention. He was again smoking his pipe and felt once more a spectator witnessing extraordinary things in a strange land. Of course, he had read Spanish books while in England, portraying the habits and characteristics of his people, but books about a land which is remote from us are not convincing. Yes, there was no doubt now, his own brother was a *chulo*. Really, there was such a profession in Spain, there were real men in Spain yet. Then there were women like La Pelos and Lunarito, women generous in their love and even in their profession, not ashamed to show their passions publicly, proud of their sex weakness, taking their inferiority as an honor, because they were not afraid to admit to themselves that they needed a man. How different from the country he had just left. And Pepe, smoking his pipe, felt for his brother the admiration of a tourist.

When he concentrated again on his uncle, the latter was already taking his coat and hat.

"Let us go, it is late. I have had a terrible day and need some sleep."

Pepe followed his uncle. Their feet made no noise as they reeled over the carpeted floor. Their shadows shrank and concentrated as they receded from the candle. Everything had the appearance of unreality, of the hidden mockery of a guignolesque farce. When they emerged from the Casino, the night was black, not a single star shone in that usually lucid sky of Madrid.

Standing before the door, they spoke:

"We had better take one of the Casino coaches, uncle?"

"You had better take it, my boy, I am walking home."

"Walking home in this darkness? Uncle, you are sure to be held up."

From the plump Prefect there issued a sneer of contempt. He raised his hand to his armpit in true *torero* style:

"No mother has yet borne the man who will have enough *pantalones* to hold me up. I am the only person in Madrid who has not been robbed. As the Prefect of Police, I must walk home when other people are too afraid to leave their houses. I could not possibly acknowledge certain things, don't you know?"

Pepe knew; he knew that after all that had happened, his uncle had an overwhelming desire to assert himself.

"I will walk part of the way with you, I am also walking home."

The Prefect rested his hand on his nephew's arm.

"They will hold you up, as soon as you leave me."

Really, this boastfulness of Don Benito portrayed him as a true Madrileño to the core. He was speaking in the best Spanish style.

And the sneer came this time from Pepe. He also raised his hand to his armpit and his uncle noticed it too because that was the arm he was holding:

"The forefathers of the man who will hold me up have not yet begun hostilities. If anyone should attempt such a reckless act, I would simply spank him and send him to Mama."

"We were always right in calling you El Españolito." His uncle laughed delightedly. He felt that he was beginning to grow fond of his nephew again, and, swept by a sudden cheerfulness, he advanced:

"Shall we make a bet?"

"Go ahead."

"A thousand pesetas if you are not robbed tonight."

"The deal is closed," cried Pepe quickly without stopping to consider that he did not own the thousand pesetas and that he might be robbed. Decidedly he was growing more and more Spanish. Almost with alarming celerity. "What about your getting robbed, uncle?"

This time the Prefect laughed openly.

"That is out of the question, my boy."

They walked up the street of Alcala. At the intersection of Peligros there was a very faint glow coming from candlelight in the Café Fornos which stood on that corner. And it was there that they decided to separate.

"Well, Pepe, good luck to you. You had better smoke your pipe and let them think that you are a detective, in which case they are sure to hold you up."

"So long, uncle, take care of yourself and prepare the thousand pesetas."

The Prefect disappeared in the shadows of the street of Peligros and Pepe began to cross Alcala.

He had scarcely taken five steps when someone stumbled against him:

"*Usted dispense,*" the person said.

"*Igualmente,*" Pepe answered. But before he reached the center of the street a thought struck him. He fumbled in his pocket. His wallet was gone.

Without a minute's hesitation he sprang back and saw by the dim light that came from Fornos the figure of a man disappearing in the darkness. Pepe ran behind and in Peligros Street he beheld a man faintly outlined against the glow of a match. Before he reached the figure the match went out, but Pepe had gauged the distance and took a leap, holding the pipe in his right hand.[1] His left hand landed on the other man's neck and he poked the mouthpiece of the pipe in the small of the back.

The man tried to shrink from Pepe's grip, but the latter held him by the collar.

"Give me the wallet," Pepe shouted.

The other one did not wait for the request to be repeated. He produced the wallet and handed it over.

"You scoundrel," Pepe said. "For this time I will let you go with this," and he delivered a most devastating kick that landed on the other man's buttocks. At that moment a clock struck two o'clock.

Pepe heard the man running away and laughed:

"A skillful pickpocket but a poor bandit," and walked back to his *casa de huespedes* feeling rather proud of himself.

When he arrived at his room, Pepe proceeded to examine the contents of his wallet to make sure that nothing was missing. He was naturally greatly surprised (by far more surprised than the reader) at finding that the wallet was not his.

He turned it about to find some way of identifying it. It contained no personal cards, not even a monogram. Its only contents, which in those days of general thievery should have been the most important, were several bank notes to the value of five hundred pesetas.

Well, it was a strange situation. Here he had held up some innocent victim. He had turned into a holdup man. Was the influence of those

---

[1] As a matter of fact, I lighted the match to illuminate the scene momentarily and get my bearings. When I began this story I did not foresee the inconvenience of such complete darkness and that it would be extremely difficult to make my characters move properly without being able to see even the paper in front of me. However, my match went out too soon for me to ascertain much, but not for Pepe Bejarano to take action, and now everything is dark again and the characters will have to be left to their own resources, meanwhile waiting until tomorrow brings the consequences to light.

days forcing itself into people's actions? Was Madrid wrapping him in its dark circumstances in order to turn him into a crook, like everybody else? Pepe laughed. No, he was an honest person and would not be tempted. The next day he was going to take the wallet to his uncle, should anybody claim it, a remote possibility in those days of skepticism.

But then again, what had become of his wallet? Someone had stolen it for sure. Was this a way in which Providence was compensating him? Was this a law of compensation which had descended upon Madrid to defend its inhabitants, when the police could not or cared not to perform its duty? This wallet contained twice as much money as his own. It was only just to keep half of it and return the other half, leaving it to this palpable Providence, whose existence was more than manifest, to compensate the owner of the wallet.

But no, Madrid, strong as it was in demoralizing people, could not eradicate so quickly the influence of so many years spent in England, and he had already argued the point with himself. It was too late. If he had only taken for granted that the wallet was his, as he had believed when he received it, it would have been all right. He could have spent the money without looking at the wallet, without admitting to himself that it was not his own (a gentleman may not be aware of the money he has). This would have been perfectly correct even in England. But now it was too late. He knew that the wallet did not belong to him. He had admitted it almost aloud even in the loneliness of his room. His only witness had been his blurred reflection in a mirror by the dim candlelight. But that was enough. Now he had to return the wallet. And Pepe, thinking how low his own funds were at the moment, wished he had never been to England.

He went to bed. He slept. In the morning he woke up and performed his ablutions, after having filled the basin that stood in the corner with cold water. The absence of hot water was annoying him. Also the absence of a bathtub. True enough, there was a tub at the other end of the passage, but it had only cold water and it was necessary to heat a tremendous amount of water to fill it. He had not realized until then how much hot water one really used in one's bath. Pepe decided to be patriotic and not take a bath, which after all cost one peseta. The peseta bounced in his brain and found its echo in the things he had heard the night before. For one peseta there was a Lunarito, perhaps more than one, in Madrid, who showed a beauty spot. The same amount that it cost to take a bath. Undoubtedly the Spaniards had a most astonishing sense of proportion. He poured some cold water over these thoughts and grumbled again. He was compensated a little later by the maid who brought him excellent chocolate with *churros*.

The maid who brought the breakfast was a twelve-year-old girl, overdeveloped even for Spain's standards of puberty. The short childish dress she wore and the socks rising from high-heeled shoes and clinging to a superbly solid pair of legs gave her an exceedingly provocative air.

Pepe saw her in the mirror. He imagined in the pronounced curve of her breasts and hips a mineralitic hardness which was communicated to him. He scented the firm youthful flesh and turned to find her looking at the opened coat of his pajamas, which exposed a hairy chest. The girl's eyes rested upon that emblem of manliness as she laid the tray with the breakfast on a chair. Pepe felt sure that he had aroused her feminine admiration. His Spanish characteristics were pushing their way out in him. He put his hands on his hips opening his pajama coat farther. There was a most persistent tremor in his throat and a certain oppression on his solar plexus. To hide this, for some people think that even in the most crudely carnal situations one must not show one's wishes too openly, if one is to attain these wishes, he did something surprisingly innocent, which showed how little he really knew about Spain. He took the towel from his shoulder and holding it open with both hands in front of him, he looked at the girl and shouted:

"*Huh, toro.*" And whirling the towel as if it were a cloak, he finished: "*Ole!*"

Had it not been for his words, his attire was so inappropriate and his style so poor even before such a charming young bull that it could not have been recognized. The girl, however, gave signs of indisputable sagacity. Always looking at his chest as if hypnotized by it, she bent forward with arms outstretched in front and charged in true bull manner. Pepe, like a real *torero,* did not move, he just turned a little and held her in his arms. Her face rested upon his naked chest and her nostrils quivered among the abundant hair.

Well, when Pepe left the *casa de huespedes* after having swallowed his cold chocolate, he was thinking of how a mere infant in Spain could teach a full-grown man so many new things. The morning was splendid, one of those typical mornings of Madrid, gay, merry, noisy and ill-smelling, sprinkled with peddlers and vendors voicing and singing their merchandise:

"El florero . . . ! Clavelitos, quien me compra claveles . . . ?"

"El afilador . . ."

"Cerezas por hierro viejo . . ."

Pepe observed that the man who was selling cherries in exchange for old iron had no more cherries left but that he continued nevertheless to voice a merchandise which did not exist. The man had accustomed his lungs to this periodical yell and if he did not let it out, he would probably explode. Pepe began to think how such a man could sleep without suddenly awaking himself with his cries, but he was interrupted in his thoughts by a beggar who accosted him.

"Caballero, una limosnita por amor de Dios."

The man had a most studied meek attitude and his appearance was ragged beyond description. He portrayed misery as one can find it only in Latin countries, if I must say so myself.

Pepe inquired:

"What is your name?"

"Laureano Baez *pa servirle caballero."*

Pepe felt happy and generous this morning and he gave the *limosnita.*

"Dios se lo pague," the beggar said, heading for another person, and Pepe thought that for once God had already paid that morning. For a flashing moment his happiness was clouded with heavy pity for this country of his, for the endless misery and poverty he had encountered since he crossed the Pyrenees. This cloud was soon dissipated by the fragrance of a violet a girl was pinning on his lapel. Pepe who felt

chatty and inquisitive that morning inquired, tilting his hat backwards and spinning his stick in his fingers as true Madrileños do under such circumstances:

"*Como te llamas?*"

"Raquel Meller," the girl laughed, holding out her hand. Decidedly his gesture had not overcome his clothes and the girl continued to believe him a foreigner.

The girl was now pinning another violet on another lapel. Pepe admired the professional volubility and ready wit of the Spanish people and as he walked toward his uncle's office he reveled in the beautiful morning.

Men sitting at the cafés discussed politics while a waiter sprayed water among the tables. Groups standing at corners interrupted now and then their perennial conversation about bullfights in order to bestow a *piropo* on a passing beauty. Young ladies with *mantillas,* but sober, black *mantillas* without a comb. And here Pepe decided to correct a false impression. Since he had arrived he had not seen a single *mantilla de madroños* or *blonda* over a comb. He had not seen flashy Spanish shawls but just black ones without embroidery. Pepe had been away from Spain long enough to expect all such things, but now he realized that the only ladies who wore these decorations were made of wax and stood in glass cases. However, he saw one or two men wearing *cordobeses* and a short jacket. And then Pepe saw what will never change in Spain. He saw that blue sky and that dazzling sun which create an exaggerated contrast between light and shadows. Shadows which are sharp, black and thick, impenetrable. And a light that is overpowering and strident.

Pepe felt in this luminous morning a sense of safety which made the dangers of the night before seem more a dream than reality. He touched his pocket. Yes, the wallet was there. He took it out to convince himself that he had not dreamed and he found himself at the office of the Prefect of Police.

Pepe entered without knocking and saw his uncle standing in front of a table, leaning on his hands, his head bowed as a bull who awaits the last blow. The table was flooded with papers.

The Prefect lifted his head and looked at his nephew sheepishly while he swept the table with a gesture.

"There you are. All letters of protest, of complaint, insulting me. . . A constant stream of letters all day long."

A boy entered with a fresh bundle of letters and laid it on top of the others. Don Benito looked at Pepe and shook his head exactly as one would do in his situation. Not even the bitter smile was missing.

Pepe felt sorry for him.

"Come on, uncle, brace up. This won't last forever. The lights will come back and peace will be reestablished."

"Hmm . . . have you come to bring me another complaint? Were you robbed last night as I predicted?"

Pepe was heroic:

"Yes, I was, I must confess it. Most clever performance, I dare say. I must apologize, however, if I cannot pay you the thousand pesetas immediately."

The Prefect waved a hand in a way that was most eloquent. While the hand moved in the air no more than a foot, it said:

"I told you so.

"It would be plain robbery to take the thousand pesetas.

"The whole thing does not matter. I am worried about more important matters now."

All this the hand said and the Prefect added:

"Pepe, I think I can trust you. . . ."

Pepe had not been long enough in Madrid to follow an eloquent hand and he misunderstood.

"Of course, uncle, you know I will pay you."

"I don't mean that, Pepe; don't be silly. I am a good uncle and never collect debts from nephews. What I mean is that I can trust you enough to make a confession."

And Pepe tried to look as much like a confessor as possible.

Don Benito continued:

"Pepe, my boy, I have been robbed. . . ."

The side of Pepe's face shrank in a sympathizing manner.

"Yes, I have been robbed. It happened last night after I left you. Five armed men fell upon me and covered me with their guns. I knew it was useless to fight. Not that I was afraid, but I owe my life to the safety of Madrid. The public depends upon my existence to protect it. I could not possibly risk a life which hardly belongs to me. Well, they went away with my wallet."

Pepe opened his mouth.

The Prefect did not let him speak.

"I don't mind the money, of course. It is the wallet I regret. Do you see? It was given to me by a certain person. I will be more frank with you; by a certain lady. This lady is very sentimental and always wants me to keep every present she gives me. I am sure that the next time I see her she will ask me if I am still using the wallet she gave me. She bases all our sentimental relations upon such trifles and I am sure that when she finds out that I no longer have the wallet it will be a disaster. She will never forgive me. If I tell her that I have lost it, she will say that I do not prize the things she gives me. If I tell her it was stolen, it will be ridiculous. And I could not tell her that it was too old and I have put it into a safe with other relics, because she gave it to me only two weeks ago. What can I do?"

Again Pepe opened his mouth to answer, but his uncle signaled him to keep quiet. His question had been purely formal.

"I was thinking of advertising, offering a reward of a thousand pesetas, but that would be exposing myself to general mockery. People would laugh. The Prefect of Police robbed! The circumstances under which the incident took place would not lessen the fact that the Prefect had been robbed. No matter how heroically I behaved in that situation, I would still be the laughingstock of all Madrid. As if a prefect were not human, as if... well, you understand. It is no use... it would..."

Pepe was standing on the other side of the table. He was bending forward with one hand on the Prefect's shoulder. In short, Pepe had assumed a protective attitude.

"At what time did you say that happened?"

"A clock struck two during the assault."

"And how much did you say the reward was?"

"A thousand pesetas . . . but as I have already told you . . ."

He did not finish. Pepe was taking something out, and there was a shrewd, a very shrewd smile on his lips:

"Is this your wallet?"

Don Benito Calinez, the man who abhorred to have people fail in situations, was perfect. He uttered without the slightest hesitation a series of the most correct and appropriate exclamations under the circumstances and then finished:

"But how did you rescue it?"

"Psss. . . . That is my business, uncle. It is one of my little secrets, don't you know? While in England I studied to be a detective under the personal supervision of Sherlock Holmes."

Don Benito, being a Prefect of Police, entertained a decided contempt for detective stories and, therefore, did not know whether Sherlock Holmes was a real person or not.

"Oh, you did? You rascal." He felt very friendly, almost crazy about his nephew and poked him in the ribs. "And you never told your uncle!"

"Well, it was a little surprise I had in store for you. That is perhaps the main reason why I was expelled from college. I did not pay enough attention to my studies, as I was most of the time helping the police. And, by the way, that is why I did not have time to recover my own wallet. I knew that yours was more important. I knew that there was a sentimental story in it."

The Prefect was really astonished.

"But how could you ever tell . . . ?"

"That is a way we detectives have of knowing things, my dear uncle."

"Well," the Prefect was effusive and dignified, "I must congratulate you. I must congratulate you, not only as a proud uncle, not only as a grateful friend who owes you a great favor, but as an admiring colleague. Tell me what can I do for you. Your uncle never forgets the good deeds of his nephews."

Pepe shrugged his shoulders in a modest way.

"Yes, Pepe, yes. I should like to write an official letter to that gentleman, to that great man—Cherlomsky, is that the name?"

"Sherlock Holmes," Pepe corrected.

"Well, I should like to write to him a letter telling that he should be proud of his pupil, that . . ."

"Oh, don't bother about that. What I have done is nothing. If I were to tell you about some of the cases I handled in England . . ."

The door opened and the boy who had brought the batch of letters entered and deposited a package before the Prefect.

Don Benito looked at the package and handed it to Pepe:

"It is for you, it was sent to my care."

Pepe opened the package. It contained a wallet which he recognized as his own. On top of the wallet there was a note written on stationery from the Café El Diamante.

The note said:

DEAR PEPE:

Sorry to have taken your wallet. I assure you it was a mistake and I am returning it to you. I do not know your address and am sending it to Uncle Benito who will give it to you. I hope you like Spain. You must have found it very changed since you left. Forgive me again. Good luck to you and if you are not too proud to accept it, receive a great embrace from your loving brother,

GASTON

P.S.—If you ever need anything do not hesitate to come to me. You can always find me through the owner of El Diamante.

Again Pepe felt the same tremor in his throat and the same oppression on his solar plexus. This time for different causes than earlier that morning.

"What a country, Spain!" he thought. "Twice in a single morning and due to the most diametrically opposed stimulants my sympathetic system has responded. Twice this morning the human has been brought out in me by this emotional land. The thing has been aroused in me which starts us living and makes us want to keep on going." And

Pepe folded the note inside his wallet and put it in his pocket.

"Well, uncle, shall we have lunch together? I suppose you feel happier now. I also feel quite happy."

"Let me rest a bit, my boy. I have had too much lately." And the Prefect sank in his chair but came up again slowly with pain reflected in his features. He was terribly sore still.

Chinelato

I

The Ogre

THERE ARE INDIVIDUALS WHOSE LIFE IS SO FULL OF ADVENTURE AND
action that it seems to be elastic in order to hold so many incidents
without bursting; incidents which in themselves would suffice to fill
the lives of many; incidents, many of which have often a secondhand
romantic flavor belonging to a past, ready-made age.

Such was the case of a certain person who once lived in the suburbs
of Madrid, in the street of Ayala, to be more exact.

At ten o'clock in the morning there was his landau standing before
his house with a coachman and lackey dressed in irreproachable
livery. Then he came out with an exaggerated dignity and slowness.
Usually with a top hat, a light tan summer coat, which did not conceal
the lower half of check trousers, and holding a cane with an ivory
handle.

This was a regular ritual. The lackey opened the garden gate for him
and then the landau door into which the master thrust his majestic
personality.

And then, his constant audience for the summer (no one in the
group could have been more than six or seven years old) stood in a
bunch at a respectable distance and suddenly burst out in a chorus:

Alto, gordo y chato,
Juan Chinelato;
tira los garbanzos y se come al gato.

Then he would look at them with obvious annoyance, and mumble in his mustache some sentence in a language they did not understand.

But even if this unfailing reaction to an individual who emanated cosmopolitanism to such a degree lent those silent suburban streets the decided aspect of a second-rate village, such a reaction, as well as the little song, was well justified by the extraordinary person who had happened like a discordant note or a meteor in those curious incipient lives.

Juan Chinelato, or at least the gentleman who was addressed by that name, which visibly annoyed him, had rented the house in the suburbs of Madrid. As a matter of fact, he was officially known as Señor Olózaga and I don't know who invented or discovered the other name. I don't even remember how the children learned the little song which was their salutation to him whenever he hove in sight.

However, Juan Chinelato, or Señor Olózaga, was a giant. He was tall, his shoulders were phenomenally broad. In short, his whole frame was big, square and massive like that of an athlete. Then his face, too, was worthy of notice. His features were flat, his chin strong, his cold eyes pronouncedly oblique, and at that time his hair was still black, both on his head and in his drooping mustache. There was a strong suggestion of the Oriental in him which contrasted excessively with his European attire. He might have been taken for a Chinaman had it not been for his deep olive complexion. I mean olive in the literal sense, not the olive color with which we Spaniards are described, but the real color of the olive which marked this man as the type of the Malay.

Some people who had seen the inside of his house said that it was luxuriously furnished in an exotic and bizarre style, and others had seen him come out on to the balcony clad in a colorful robe and smoking a long pipe.

It was said that all by himself he could dispose of a whole roasted pig and a barrel of rum, that he was a bigamist and that his other wives had disappeared in a mysterious manner. In fact, he aroused the curiosity of the whole neighborhood and the most fantastic tales were told about him. Of course, he was not Spanish and undoubtedly the blood of all races was mixed in his veins to produce a strange and dangerous character.

All these things were more than sufficient to appeal to the imagination of children and arouse their interest and gossip, not to mention that of the grownups, and during that summer the whole neighborhood was in a fever. This individual frightened and attracted everyone, he often must have appeared in the dreams of many, sometimes like a black ogre, sometimes like a Chinese dragon, always spitting fire and devouring children.

All this, imagination invented or discovered about the person of Señor Olózaga, an eccentric and exotic gentleman who wore a colorful robe at home, smoked a long pipe sometimes, had rented a house for the summer in the suburbs of Madrid, and every morning left in his carriage and rode to the center of the city leaving behind a group of bewildered children singing in chorus:

> *Alto, gordo y chato,*
> *Juan Chinelato;*
> *tira los garbanzos y se come al gato.*

The Mission

Señor Olózaga is very fond of speaking of himself. Indeed, his life is a wonderful subject of conversation. But I am always under the impression that he keeps to himself a great deal which he leaves unsaid, and that at other times he changes the names of people and places. Much of what I know about his life I owe to him, but I also owe as much to people who have known him at different periods.

His opinion of himself and the opinion that other people have of him are at times quite diametrically opposed. While he insists that in his veins runs the blood of remote dynasties and legendary princes, other people insist that he is a common adventurer who comes from low colonial stock of pariahs and God knows what. But I say that he may be an adventurer, but not at all common. I really don't know what his race or races may be, but I know that he is a Spanish citizen and travels under such a passport. I am under the impression that he has as many enemies as he has friends and he can make friends easily. I believe that many envy him his innate ability to make a success of his life, that he can show pictures in which he appears with the royalty and high lights of Europe, that he speaks almost every language in existence fluently, that he lives like a prince and spends a tremendous amount of money. He is much of a showman and slightly cynical, but on the whole he is a jolly good fellow.

The origin of his life is obscure. Neither he nor anybody else has been able to enlighten me as to who his father and mother were. There are vague memories of one day when as an infant he arrived at a house in front of which people were gathered. When he entered he saw a dead woman lying on the floor. Then someone came in and took him away.

After that there is the memory of riding for a day and a night and then another day upon marshy land and seeing rice fields and men and women toiling in them, and snowy mountains in the distance. All this accompanied by the proximity of a gentleman with a thick beard and smelling strongly of tobacco. Then comes a recollection of waking up in a bed and the man with the beard coming into the room and leading him into another larger chamber, where there were more men with thick beards, also smelling strongly of tobacco. After that he ate rice with milk and remembers the taste of chocolate for the first time in his life. He was led into a garden and saw other children playing.

All his recollections of that time are confused. He does not remember whether it was that afternoon, or some days after, when he was in a large hall with colored glass windows, at the end of which there was a large stand covered with white material. There stood figures of men and women dressed mainly in red and blue robes with gilded rings about their heads and many candles which a bearded man was lighting.

Then he found himself held over a marble basin while water was poured over his head. There was speaking in a monotonous voice, and soft music coming from above. From that day he was called Juan Chinelato.

He remained some time among these people and found himself speaking Spanish. They taught him the catechism and mathematics and geography, and thus he found out that this place belonged to a larger place known as the Chinese Empire. These people taught him also to help with the Mass and he was able to say several sentences in Latin. He learned to swing the incensory and steal now and then a drink or two from the holy wine decanter.

Twice every month he was taken into a dark booth, where he met the same thick beard and strong smell of tobacco, and he was asked the same questions, which he always answered as best he could. He was told to recite such and such prayers. Invariably the next day before breakfast he was led in a row with other children to the end of the hall, where the many candles were, and another thick beard smelling of tobacco gave them a tasteless wafer to swallow.

Then one night, when he must have been about ten years old, there was great confusion all over the place. Voices were heard and also the noise made by gunshots. He and other children got out of bed half asleep and wandered into the corridors. There they beheld much disorder. The monks were going to and fro with guns in their hands. They leaned against the windows and shot into the darkness. Juan Chinelato was not afraid, he was just curious. While the other children cringed in a corner, he walked boldly down the stairs and found the main hall barricaded and more monks with guns at the windows.

Then he heard outside voices, strange voices in the night that brought back memories of another night and a huge house whose front was illuminated red by the glow of a bonfire, and then a white man fighting Chinamen in that red light and a woman screaming inside the house. These memories swept him with irresistible force, awaking in him an unknown self of wild and heroic deeds, which he had often imagined in his sleepless nights. Something stirred within him that drew him to a window and he looked outside and heard the voices more clearly and detonations in the darkness. Something crashed against the window and everything went black.

When he woke up he was riding at breakneck speed upon a horse, held tightly between two strong arms. He felt dizzy and as he lifted his head his cheek came in contact with a thick beard and his nostrils perceived the well-known odor of tobacco. Then a voice said:

"How does your head feel?"

He looked up and saw the same monk who had taken him on his first ride some years ago. He went on to explain that there had been an uprising of Chinese bandits who had attacked the mission, killed almost everyone and set the building on fire. Juan had been wounded and the monk had succeeded in taking a horse and escaping with him through the Chinese lines.

Juan put a hand to his head and felt a bandage. The night was now clear, almost dazzling, and there was an enormous moon like those painted on Chinese screens. Again Juan saw the marshy land and rice fields, vast silver plains, and in the distance he also saw the snowy mountains against the sky. And he remembers riding like wind in the night and then going back to sleep.

That dazzling night of adventure formed the background of his life.

Adventure

Around the age of sixteen or eighteen the strength of Juan Chinelato must have been already quite worthy of notice.

He is known to have been rowing on some kind of convict ship where the convicts were chained to the benches.

Juan Chinelato was talking to the man rowing in front of him when the guard approached.

"You horrible monkey," he yelled. "I will teach you to keep your mouth shut and attend to your job." And he gave him a terrible blow with his whip upon the naked back.

This was the first time that Juan Chinelato had been so brutally insulted in public and he flattered himself that no man had done so with impunity in his life. His cold eyes flashed like two burning coals. He let go the oar and with a single pull both the chain and bench were torn and broken. Then he turned upon the frightened guard, who had no time to call for help, and with one blow of the thick chain he brought him down dead, his head split open like a melon.

All the men about him were silent with awe at the sudden tragedy. Juan Chinelato was lost. Other watchmen were coming armed with guns and knives. There was only one thing to do and Juan Chinelato did it. With a phenomenal leap he went overboard and disappeared under the water, in a sea alive with sharks.

The watchmen shot once or twice just as a matter of formality and then turned around to reestablish order, knowing that soon justice would be done anyway.

But this was one of the many times that justice was not accomplished in the life of Chinelato. An unfailing good luck, combined with his herculean constitution and an infinite reserve of energy, carried him successfully through a life that would have done away with ten ordinary men. He drifted during two consecutive days until he was picked up by a merchant ship that crossed between China and the Philippine Islands and whose skipper, a Spaniard of ill repute, had underhanded dealings in opium and other smuggled goods.

His physical strength must have won him the respect and good will of the new crew and its skipper. After the labors of the day, when supper had been consumed and the sailors sat around to watch the sun set behind the horizon, they would organize wrestling matches in which Juan Chinelato invariably came out the victor.

His popularity and fame as a strong man soon broadened and at every port they touched he met the strongest men from other crews and easily defeated them, until he won the undisputed title of Champion of the China Sea.

During all this time he had gained influence over his captain. At that time he already spoke Spanish, Chinese and several dialects. This, together with his quick intelligence, ready wit and elastic conscience, must have made him appear a priceless asset to the old skipper, who began to consider him his right hand in all sorts of shady dealings.

All that is known of this part of his life is that, together with the captain, he cruised all those seas and islands and that with him he made his first fortune; that one day, after having been gone for some time, he reappeared in Mindanao without the captain, in full command of the ship and with another crew. At the first port he sold both ship and crew and established himself in Manila.

There he took to drinking and leading a riotous life. . . . His two main weaknesses had been gambling and women, and both things nearly dissolved his fortune in less than two years. Again he found himself almost in misery, but he was not a man to worry over such trifles. He was entirely too popular, good or bad, his reputation was established in that part of the world and he had too many good connections to be long without a fortune. Therefore, he squared his shoulders and prepared himself to seek new adventure.

A Vision

One afternoon, as Chinelato was going in his carriage toward La Luneta, he saw one of the few women whom he really loved in his life.

It was a sudden and unexpected vision that for a moment disturbed all his mental faculties. She went by in her light carriage completely dressed in white, but her dress as well as her golden curls and snowy complexion were deeply tinted with the pink glow coming from a red parasol she held over her head and that of an elderly lady who sat by her side, and the red reflection turned her great blue eyes into two wonderful purple amethysts.

Chinelato did not notice the details. He was just struck by the whole of this fleeting vision of gold and red that led away into the sunset enveloped in a cloud of *ilan-ilan* and *sampaguita*. He literally turned around inside his carriage and leaned against the folded top as if it were a window, his mouth open, his eyes following the red parasol receding in the distance like a poppy carried by the wind in the afternoon glow.

The gentleman who sat beside him pulled him by the sleeve and said in a bland voice:

"*Le gusta,* Señor Chinelato?"

"Who . . . is . . . that?" he inquired, not yet quite recovered from the impression.

"She is Señorita Bejarano, the only daughter of Don Esteban Bejarano y Ulloa, a government employee here."

"Well, she is the most beautiful creature I have seen, even if she is the daughter of a government employee."

"Why, Señor Chinelato, I thought you were past the stage of looking at beautiful ladies. You are a married man."

"You know very well how much marriage stands in the way of love in these countries. . . . Really, that girl is just simply marvelous and if I . . ."

"But your wife is very beautiful, too, Señor Chinelato. . . ."

Juan Chinelato was always greatly annoyed at people bringing up objections to things he liked.

"If you find my wife so beautiful, take her!" he said brutally.

The other man raised his eyebrows slightly but again smiled softly.

"What things you say, Señor Chinelato."

"What the devil? I speak what I think and say it clearly. My wife does not interest me any longer. I seek my amusement elsewhere. It is just that she gets someone who will love her oftener than I do, provided it is not a priest."

The other man laughed.

"Certainly. I don't mind being a cuckold, but I refuse to be the provider of a priest. What the devil? They are the regular home-wreckers in this land. There is not a single home here where they have not smuggled their little bastard in some corner. They live on the fat of the land . . . and you know how much I like the fat ladies."

"Yes. Señorita Bejarano is rather plump and well developed for her age."

At the mention of this name Chinelato went into a reverie. He seemed to be talking to himself and mentally smacking his tongue. He remained silent a while and then ended aloud:

". . . yes, she is a capital female!" and went back into his reverie and spoke no more during the rest of the drive.

When he woke from his thoughts the carriage was standing still and the other man was asking him to dine in his company.

Chinelato excused himself and said good-by. When the coachman was beginning to turn toward his home, he touched him on the shoulder with his cane and said:

"Drive for an hour or so anywhere. I don't care what direction you choose, just keep going and then take me to the house of Don Esteban Bejarano." And he leaned back on the cushions and closed his eyes.

And for a long time he remained in the same position without opening his eyes until his carriage stopped at the residence of Don Esteban Bejarano y Ulloa.

II

The Black Mandarin

"So you knew The Black Mandarin?"

"I never met him personally but I have heard of him."

"He was a novelistic character and I can't help admiring him. With more men of his caliber, perhaps Spain might not have lost the Philippines to the United States when it did."

"Psss. . . . I don't know about that. Perhaps with more men of his caliber Spain might have lost the Philippines to the natives. Perhaps, without the United States, he might have ended by owning the whole country. He practically ruled there . . . and that with enemies on both sides of the fence."

"Yes, he was a strong character and at that time the most influential man there. They were afraid of him. He knew mankind entirely too well."

"He had money and he knew the price of men. In his dealings with Spanish authorities he said that if he wanted to convince a man, he set down a pile of gold and then he added more gold to it, and as the pile grew taller the man grew weaker, until the pile collapsed and the man fell, too. He was a philosopher and a cynic also."

"Yes, every man had a price there, but once he failed. True, it was

111

not precisely a matter of politics but rather a personal question, and that was the first time that he did not get what he had set out to win. It was also the first time that he could not get revenge. . . . But perhaps you have not heard of that incident?"

"I have a vague recollection."

One day The Black Mandarin called at the residence of Don Esteban Bejarano y Ulloa.

When he was announced, Don Esteban failed to register the natural surprise that this exceptional visit should have caused him. The Black Mandarin was not in the habit of calling on any of the Spanish authorities; he rather deigned to receive them at his own palace where he entertained them in a condescending and royal manner.

However, Don Esteban Bejarano y Ulloa apparently was not surprised. Not even when The Black Mandarin appeared before him. The Black Mandarin was known to dress invariably in his native costume, costly garments of a subdued exterior which now and then allowed glimpses of a dazzling lining. But this day The Black Mandarin was attired in an immaculate white suit, closed to the neck, the whiteness of which made his gigantic figure seem larger still, and he held a cork hat in one hand and a small collapsible fan in the other. But for his face and hands, The Black Mandarin looked as European as possible.

For the third time I say that Don Esteban Bejarano y Ulloa was not surprised. He merely advanced a few steps to meet his guest and said

"Oh, Señor Chinelato! To what do I owe the honor of this visit?"

The Black Mandarin bowed and shook hands in the best European manner but his face, still as the surface of a pond, never rippled under the suggestion of a smile.

Don Esteban motioned him to a settee and then sat himself on a chair facing him and from a near table took a *pay-pay* and began to fan himself slowly.

Although outside the day was scorching hot as usual, a certain degree of coolness prevailed in the chamber where the two men sat. The drawn shades gave a refreshing and pronounced shade that len everything, especially the pale face of Don Esteban, a greenish hue. The two men fanned themselves rhythmically and in silence. Then, through the porch and from some other chamber, the notes of a melody played upon a piano came to increase the calmness of the moment.

Don Esteban Bejarano y Ulloa spoke again:

"Yes, Señor Chinelato, it was fortunate that you came today. Tomorrow my fever is due at this time and I would have been deprived of this pleasure."

The Black Mandarin seemed distracted. Either he was listening to the music or thinking of the times when other men more important than the one sitting before him had come to him shaking with fever and hardly able to walk, because The Black Mandarin had never been known to postpone an interview in order to accommodate a man.

Don Esteban was carrying on the conversation:

"Yes, this periodic fever is very annoying. . . . That is my daughter playing."

The Black Mandarin shut his fan as if closing a cadenza of the melody.

"Señor Bejarano, for some time I have tried to discuss with you a matter which you have most persistently put off." His Spanish was quite perfect. There was not in his pronunciation a single *l* instead of an *r*. It rather sounded like that of a Latin American. "Today I have come to get a definite answer. I have come to ask you for the hand of your daughter."

Don Esteban missed two strokes with his fan and then went on without answering. The Black Mandarin followed the fan with his oblique, frozen eyes. Don Esteban counted five strokes and then said:

"Señor Chinelato, I appreciate the honor and I feel sure that my daughter will appreciate it, too." There was a slight mockery in the voice of Don Esteban. The music had ceased in the other room. "Señor Chinelato, you do not understand."

The Black Mandarin did not choose to understand.

"Of course, Señor Bejarano, there must always be some objections in a question of this nature . . . after all, it is the fashion." The Black

113

Mandarin was cynical, perhaps slightly insulting. Don Esteban continued to fan himself placidly.

"Señor Chinelato, I do not doubt that you are aware of that over-rated intuition in women which is supposed to make up for all the other spiritual qualities they lack. . . . Well, do not think for a moment that I am taking the liberty of talking for myself. My daughter told me this morning that in the eventuality of your honoring us with a call and a proposal, she authorized me to refuse in her name. . . . Otherwise, Señor Chinelato, I would have referred you to her."

From the other room now came the notes of the Rondeau Capriccioso of Mendelssohn.[1] The scintillating phrases chased each other in a gay, humorous manner. The Black Mandarin straightened up:

"But what are the objections, Señor Bejarano? Undoubtedly your daughter has been a little hasty. I am an influential man, I have position. To speak very frankly and without flattering myself, I can say that I am a very desirable catch. Decidedly your daughter has not thought of my influence and position. . . ."

"Señor Chinelato, it is unnecessary to prolong this painful situation further. I thank you in my name and in that of my daughter, and do believe that I regret to be compelled to refuse the first thing you have asked of me since I have had the privilege of knowing you."

The Black Mandarin was beginning to lose his patience. There were reasons why a man like himself should not expect this refusal and should act so persistently. He said:

"But I am willing to wait. I cannot hope to be accepted by your daughter immediately, although I do not see why I shouldn't. But let us grant that some people need time to make up their minds. All I ask is to be allowed to call on your daughter, to talk to her, to see her . . . and hope like a man in love and a gentleman."

"It is useless, Señor Chinelato . . . you do not understand . . . you do not seem to want to understand. . . . You see, Señor Chinelato? My daughter is white."

---

[1] To tell the truth, the character in the other room did not know how to play this composition and insisted on playing an inadequate popular dance throughout this scene, but this is one time I am determined to have my way and we shall have the more appropriate Rondeau instead.

Although The Black Mandarin was sitting with his back to a shaded window and his features were in darkness, Don Esteban saw his eyes sparkle. There was a long silence during which The Black Mandarin looked at his hands and his powerful chest swelled. A wind of savagery brushed his mind in forgotten visions which came back with irresistible clearness. In his mind he saw the front of a house illuminated by the red glow of a bonfire and a white man fighting Chinamen, and then he heard clearly the screams of a woman and he felt a lash on his bare back and saw himself at the oar in a convict ship. His chest sank and swelled again and his eyes, now frozen, descended once more upon his hands.

Don Esteban continued:

"I am infinitely sorry to mention that fact but . . ."

The Black Mandarin made a motion with his closed fan in the air: a conventional gesture of forgiveness to his interlocutor which his expression denied. In the other room the music sounded again. After a short pause the theme of the Rondeau had reappeared rolling on the keyboard as the laughing echo of a comic phrase alternating with ample chords, too persuasive, too impertinent. The Black Mandarin rose.

"I expected this much from a man of your type, but I am surprised that you should fail to realize the convenience of my proposal to both your daughter and yourself. You are just a fool clogged with old-fashioned ideas and prejudices."

Don Esteban put his *pay-pay* down and also rose.

"Señor Chinelato, I believe I have exceeded myself in politeness. Now I must beg you to spare me the unpleasantness of your presence."

The Black Mandarin picked up his hat from the settee.

"I have also exceeded myself in patience if not in politeness, Señor Bejarano, and let me tell you that I am well aware of your situation, a situation which you have refused to better though holding a position which enabled you to do so, and that now with a stupid racial prejudice you are turning out a man in whose veins circulates the blood of the highest dynasties, a man who could have saved you from utter ruin and made your daughter happy."

115

"Make my daughter happy? Señor Chinelato! I may be a fool but not to that degree. Even if my daughter were to accept you, even if the racial prejudice did not exist, all of which is going too far in a hypoth esis, I would refuse, sir, I would refuse. . . . Don't I, as well as everybody else, know your past history? I could ask you: what became of your firs wife, and your second wife? Señor Chinelato, you are mad if you ever dream that I could thrust my only daughter into the hands of a man like you. . . . Undoubtedly you are not in your right senses."

The mocking phrases of the Rondeau had broadened now into a deep melody only to return abruptly to their jesting play.

"No, I am not. I have not been since the first day I saw your daughter . . . Yes, I have been mad, I have thought of nothing else, and no matter what a man may have been, is he to be denied the right to be in love? have come here full of sincerity and the best sentiments. . . . I have come to lay my fortune, my honor, my name, everything I have at the feet of your daughter, and I meet with insolent mockery, with an insulting attitude and even my race is thrown in my face as a stigma. . . ." His hand tightened and the fan fell to the floor, broken like a crushed withered flower.

"Señor Chinelato, I repeat that you do not understand, that you refuse to understand. . . ."

From the other room came stridently a false note and the music wa interrupted. Then the merry phrase was resumed with difficulty, like a badly told joke, more offensive in its awkwardness. The Black Mandarin said:

"I understand, sir; fortunately, I have regained my senses. This is no the first time that you have displeased me. I have been entirely too lenient with you but, by Christ! I will run you out of this country.'

Don Esteban Bejarano y Ulloa was inimitable. He bowed slightly and said in a suave manner:

"I am very sorry that I cannot oblige you even in that. I have already presented my resignation. My health is impaired by this climate and am returning to Spain with my family. Good afternoon, Seño Chinelato."

The Black Mandarin stood there looking at Don Esteban. He felt strong impulse to crush this man. Then he pushed his hat on his head and rushed out.

As he was crossing the garden he heard a boy's voice coming from a window:

"Who is that ugly Chinaman?"

And then a feminine voice:

"Keep quiet, Gil."

He felt the blood mount to his head and a foul epithet escape him. He had felt again the lash upon his bare back.

At the gate he heard a powerful bark and a voice crying in Filipino dialect. He turned around and saw a huge dog rushing toward him with a piece of torn leash hanging from his neck and a little Tagalo running behind.

The Black Mandarin planted himself firmly. He raised his hands and awaited the attack. The dog took a leap and the powerful hands of Chinelato closed like claws about his neck. For a moment it was the fight of an animal with another animal. The dog tore away and wriggled, but in vain; the viselike grip grew stronger and stronger, the iron fingers bored through and sank into the dog's neck mercilessly. The face of Chinelato glowed with savage joy. He kept the dog hanging in that way and his hold tightened further. The dog grew limp. Then a woman was heard screaming inside the house and Chinelato released his hold. The dog fell to the ground like a rag.

Both the little Tagalo and his own coachman had witnessed the scene without uttering a word, trembling with fear. The Black Mandarin entered his carriage and said to the coachman:

"Drive for an hour or so anywhere, I don't care what direction you choose, just keep going and then . . . take me home." And he leaned back on the cushions and closed his eyes.

"And what became of Señorita Bejarano and The Black Mandarin?"

"She returned to Spain with her family and married a wealthy merchant, and as to The Black Mandarin, for some time he was thought dead, assassinated. He had disappeared just before the United States took possession of the Philippines. But then some people learned that he was alive . . . and you know? That man who had been so influential came to Spain shoveling coal in a ship."

"I did not know that. His life was certainly full of contrasts, he was a colorful character. They say that his house in Manila was the most sumptuous palace, that people visited it as a museum."

"Hmmm. . . . He was a very interesting man. Let's have another drink."

The Plantation

Juan Chinelato did not stay in Spain very long the first time. He went away soon.

From a man who said he knew all about him I learned that he spent some time in the West Indies and Mexico and later somewhere in South America. Cuba, however, seemed to be the most propitious country for him. There he made a fortune in sugar plantations and in white slavery. The man who said he knew all about him entertained obviously a bad opinion of Chinelato mixed with apparent admiration. From him I learned that when Chinelato first arrived at Cuba from Spain he did not have a cent to his name. He went to work at a sugar plantation owned by a rich Basque called Iturbe. There he soon commanded the respect of his fellow workers because of his physical strength and his ability to outdrink everybody with rum. Always fond of gambling, he gambled with the other men and in that way managed to add to his scanty pay.

One day Señorita Iturbe came to look at the plantation with her father. There she saw Chinelato for the first time. She stopped her horse while her father advanced, talking to a foreman, and for a long time admired the giant. Chinelato was stripped from his waist up. She was amazed. Under his bronze skin, glittering with perspiration at the tropical sun, his muscles gathered into bulky masses, protruded and then scattered into thick knots rolling all over his enormous frame like waves in a dark sea. She also noticed his drooping mustache and his dull oblique eyes, which lent him the enigmatic aspect of a disdainful faun.

Señorita Iturbe returned often and stopped her horse on the same spot and looked long and dreamily at Chinelato. She was pale, with a strong tendency to anemia and persistently read the poems of Campo Amor.

Chinelato looked at her as an equal, perhaps as an inferior, and sometimes he did not look at her at all.

According to the man who knows all about it, she looked as if saying: "I know you want to and I also want to, but it is impossible."

But Chinelato made it possible. They gazed at the same colossal moon hanging from a low and brilliant sky, and he thought of marshy lands and rice fields and fancied snowy mountains in the distance, and she thought of him and mentally recited the poems of Campo Amor. And then they scented and drank the same fresh, strong coffee and she played *danzones* and he sang *guajiras,* and the same ripe mangos melted in their mouths. Indeed, he made it possible and one night he carried her away.

The Champion

The next thing he was in Havana, married to Señorita Iturbe. She was no longer anemic, but she had contracted other affections and still read Campo Amor. As to Chinelato, he engaged in several wrestling exhibitions and then won the championship.

As champion, Chinelato shone once more in the public eye. He was colorful, an accomplished showman, and knew how to do things well. At a wrestling exhibition or match he always appeared wrapped in a luxurious and elegant Chinese robe and had Waldteufel's Skaters Waltz played by the orchestra, and smiled, displaying a row of wonderfully white teeth. He was a favorite with the public. The fact that he was married to a white woman and beginning to get tired of her added greatly to his notoriety and the public admiration.

Then he went to the United States for a professional engagement. He was successful there, too, and married another white lady. But his former wife, who followed him everywhere, with or without his consent, and who, according to the man who knew it all, was crazy about him, made a terrible scandal in New York and he left the country on a charge of bigamy.

He returned to Havana and then gave himself to a licentious exis-tence. With a group of friends he would run through the city late at night creating a row in every café, on every corner, his strength and wealth becoming more and more insulting. He had never forgiven his wife for the turn she played him in New York and now he ill-treated her in the most cruel manner.

The man who knew all about it told me that by that time Chinelato practically owned a small street in a quarter of Havana, until then rather obscure. There he had installed cafés, amusement places and some other places where one could procure drugs or any other particular thing which might not be legal. There he could be seen drunk every night carrying on with prostitutes and all kinds of gay people.

His wife was pregnant by this time and with the life he led her in that condition she looked very old and sickly. The man who knew used to tell me that it was a shame that an aristocratic white lady like her had run herself to death for such a nigger.

One night she came to the street looking for her husband to get some money from him.

He was drunk as usual. He took her brutally by the arm and placed her in front of two painted ladies who were sitting at his table:

"Look at them and look at yourself. When you can do what they can, come to me for money. Now kneel before your superiors and then get out!"

In the condition in which she was she had to kneel before the two women and then go away amid general mirth.

Madame Chinelato gave birth to a baby. Her husband immediately seized this opportunity to mortify her. He began to say that the child was not his own. He hired one of his stablemen to claim that he was the real father.

The man who knows says:

"As a matter of fact, people who saw the baby said that he was the living image of Chinelato, and not a single person, not even his friends who knew him and his wife, doubted for a moment but that this was his legitimate son. However, they laughed at the joke and thought it was very clever of him to say that and make himself out publicly a cuckold."

When his wife became more used to his accusations about the legitimacy of the baby he took to mortifying her in another manner.

He would go on the balcony with the infant and then toss him up into space, right over the street, saying: "Jump, little bastard, jump!" and kept this game up until the child began to cry. The poor mother watched, paralyzed with panic, not daring to say or do anything, lest he should let the baby fall.

When I heard this I asked:

"And why did she not take the baby and go away with it?"

And for once the man who knew it all seemed to hesitate:

"Well . . . I don't know what kind of fascination that man exercised over her that she became his slave."

For some reason Chinelato delighted in making his wife suffer. Once on the anniversary of their wedding, Chinelato acted very affably toward his wife; he had been exaggeratedly kind to her for the whole week and she feared, because these moods usually heralded one of his refined cruelties. On this particular anniversary he went beyond his usual limit of kindness toward her.

Chinelato was known to be very fond of roast pork; he often ate a whole suckling all by himself and on this occasion he dismissed all the servants and told his wife that he was going to roast a whole pig and serve personally the dinner so that they would not be disturbed and could have a second private honeymoon. The poor woman was overcome with all this. He gave her carte blanche, and the afternoon of that day she went shopping.

When she returned home she missed the baby but her husband told her not to worry, that he had a special surprise for her. Dinner was served and Madame Chinelato sat at the table not knowing what to think.

Chinelato entered wearing an apron and a cook's cap, carrying a huge silver platter with a cover like a dome. He was in a very happy mood, taking insinuating dance steps, laughing and showing a row of wonderfully white teeth.

He set the platter before his wife. He sat down facing her and told her to open it.

When she uncovered it she grew livid as a corpse, her mouth gaping, her eyes protruding, and then very slowly she collapsed without uttering a single sound, still holding the cover in her hand, while Chinelato laughed long and loud at his own joke in the lonely house.[1]

This terrible shock finished poor Madame Chinelato. She lost her reason completely. For three days she sat with her eyes fixed in space, then she would move a hand as if uncovering something and burst out into horrible screams. For three days and nights she was in that condition. She refused to eat and no one was able to feed her anything, and the last night, when Chinelato left his home, he saw in the street a group of boys who had built a bonfire.

The front of his house was illuminated with a red glow. He called to the boys to go away and then chased them down the street. Inside the house the insane woman was screaming and she died that night.

When I heard this weird incident, I could not help thinking that it was a bit melodramatic and overdone. I said:

"But that was a crime. What about the authorities? Didn't they do something about it?"

And the man who knew all hesitated again:

"Well . . ." he said.

The Butterfly Charmer

After his wife's death Chinelato went on with his gay life. He married

---

[1] Several persons have objected to this passage which they find distasteful to say the least, among others my friend Dr. José de los Rios, and such characters as Madame Chinelato and the baby in question. I also objected to it, but Chinelato insisted upon being very evil at this point in the story. It is not my fault if, although personally preferring to have actual roast pork, Chinelato should prove unyielding in his culinary prerogatives. Besides like all stage dinners this is a make-believe one and the platter really held a cardboard dummy.

a woman he had met in his street and then proceeded to drink and gamble. His street, lacking in proper management, soon began to lose. When he was drunk he always insisted on paying for everything that had been consumed; he invited guests to everything and with all this he soon squandered his fortune.

Soon after that came the loss of his championship. The match was staged in Havana and his opponent was a white man still more of a giant and before whom even Chinelato looked rather small.

Some people say that Chinelato, due to the life he had led, was in poor condition for this match and had not trained at all. Others say, among them the man who knows all about him, that he sold himself for a large sum of money, that his opponent, though big, was a flabby man who could not compare with Chinelato in strength or in technique, that Chinelato played with him for a long time to give the public a good show and then lay on the floor of his own accord, pushed the hands of his opponent against his own shoulders and even winked at some of his friends in the audience.

The fact remains that after he lost his championship he had a lot of money and then he went to Spain, and in the company of his other white wife he toured the country triumphantly.

From that time dates, I believe, his assumption of the name of Olózaga. As Señor Olózaga, he owned a circus which played in several Spanish cities. In this circus he performed also, not as an athlete but as a butterfly trainer.

I remember seeing him when his circus was in San Sebastian. In the mornings he appeared on the beach clad in a rich robe. All his life he showed a marked preference for beautiful robes. Then, standing before the water, he would let the robe fall into the respectful hands of a perennially awestricken valet and display his magnificent physique to everybody.

The women admired him and swarmed about him like butterflies, and he permitted himself a number of liberties with them, always smiling and showing a row of white teeth: liberties that would never have been granted to the rickety gentlemen with monocles, who looked on disgustedly from a distance.

After that he took his morning swim and entertained himself playing with the children, holding them with one hand and tossing them into the water as if they were balls. On these occasions he never struck me as the man who has been described, but rather as a kind gentleman, fond of children.

I also remember seeing his act at his circus. I was very curious to see it. According to people, he had trained the butterflies to such a degree that he made them do anything he pleased. He led them with a fan and they flew all over the place or stood close to him and did a multitude of clever things. The most sensational part of the act, however, was at the end, when his fan quivered slightly but rapidly and all the butterflies stood above it in a semicircle, fluttering their wings and spelled his name. He was supposed to be the only man who could perform this act. Some people said that the butterflies were not real.

I was in the front row the night I saw him perform. He came out in a magnificent mandarin coat, holding a great fan in his hand. In the center of the stage there was a table with a box and a small xylophone.

The orchestra began to play a waltz.

Chinelato opened his fan with a magnificent gesture, closed it and opened it again with graceful and rhythmic motions in time with the music. Then he opened the box and taking a small padded hammer struck upon a key of the xylophone, which harmonized with the orchestra: a butterfly sprang out of the box and landed right on the edge of his fan. He struck another key and another butterfly came out in the same manner and alighted beside her sister. He repeated this seven times, going through the whole scale always in harmony with the music, and then, with one motion he ran upwards through the keys of the xylophone and a swarm of butterflies sprang up from the box and filled the stage, flying all over the place. Then he ran downwards through all the keys and the music ceased, and all the butterflies hovered about him, alighted upon the fan, his arms and shoulders. He was covered with butterflies.

Then the waltz began again and slowly he began to work his fan in time with the waltz. It flapped like a wing. It was a beautiful performance to watch. He gathered the butterflies in a big bunch and then scattered them in groups, in pairs, in trios. It was marvelous, the docility with which they followed the enchanted fan. Like a battalion he led them in columns of four abreast or in long double columns and made them go through all the motions of a well-trained army. They went to and fro rhythmically following the fan as if it were a huge butterfly, sometimes undulating slowly as something that is falling asleep and then flapping furiously in a sudden awakening. They circled about him, then descended almost to the stage floor and, as the fan rose, they went up high into the air.

He was a real artist and went through all the motions of a dance in perfect time with the waltz, turning, sliding over the stage, guiding his butterflies, his coat opening about him like another fan and disclosing a golden interior, his great figure and his impassive features illuminated by the footlights, as if the stage were an altar, as if it were a ritual dance petrified into eternity by the action of time.

At last the moment came when we were about to witness the almost miraculous performance of the butterflies spelling his name.

I sat all attention, but I was not destined to see that extraordinary part of the program. There was a silence in the music. The orchestra ceased playing and the pianist began the Rondeau Capriccioso of Mendelssohn.

At first I thought that this contrast was intended as a finale for the performance, but to my great astonishment, the butterfly charmer signaled the pianist abruptly to stop, then he closed his fan with visible disgust and as if by enchantment all the butterflies flopped down and disappeared inside the box.

Chinelato closed the box in a general silence, then he bowed to the audience and withdrew.

As I have said, Señor Chinelato or Señor Olózaga performed in his circus in several cities in Spain. However, gambling was a mania with him and he lost a great deal of money that way. Many of his artists and performers began to complain that he did not pay them and finally the circus dissolved.

After that Señor Olózaga went to Madrid and settled down. There he dedicated himself to promoting spectacles of all kinds. Being a showman was his long suit and he knew that this was the field in which he could make money. He also began to back bad *toreros* and in this he lost a great deal of money and likewise his wife, who ran away with the *torero* he was protecting at the time.

Tia Mariquita

"But didn't you know Tia Mariquita?"

"No, I never had that pleasure."

"Well, you have missed a very curious person. Had it not been for certain discrepancies, she would have been quite a harmonious character belonging to a past age."

I don't remember the exact name of Tia Mariquita. Everybody called her that. She had a great number of nephews and relatives, close and distant.

Tia Mariquita had a wonderful imagination, she allowed herself to be carried away by it to such a degree that one could never tell truth from falsehood where she was concerned. It was due to that worthy lack of respect for exactness which characterized her that I was unable to find out about her origin or her life before the time I met her.

I remember her Sunday afternoon gatherings, a complex mixture of ordinary and extraordinary persons: South American poets, writers and actors whose works or performances no one had seen, and then an endless row of nephews and nieces. Pale shrunken-up boys prematurely old and also pale ultra-religious girls with mustaches. All of them the picture of tuberculosis bred from indoor life. I also remember the parents of these boys and girls listening to the conversation distractedly while watching their offspring intently, always on the lookout for misbehavior.

I particularly remember a lengthy stooping boy with short trousers exposing ugly hairy legs, which immediately called attention to his sullen, bearded face. This boy was on that occasion biting his nails voraciously.

His mother from the other end of the room signaled him to cease, with a gesture too vehement to pass unnoticed.

The boy shook his head doggedly and went on with more gusto than ever.

The mother, realizing that she was noticed, felt the necessity of explaining:

"He is very nervous. Lately he has taken to walking in his sleep. The other night we found him in the corridor walking toward the servants' rooms."

The boy turned as red as his deeply set anemia permitted and went on biting his nails, both hands in his mouth at a time.

"And has Dr. de los Rios recommended anything?"

"No." This was the father speaking now. "He says that it is better not to send him to bed so early, but to let him take a walk at night, that the night air will do him good and he will sleep better after that."

At these Sunday afternoon gatherings, Tia Mariquita recited poetry and accompanied herself at the piano. She was well in her sixties at that time, of a queenly carriage which she stressed zealously. Her hair was dyed in some carrot shade and her makeup cracked over her deep wrinkles. She dressed in fantastic gowns, pink or pale blue with much gold embroidery and lace and with marabou feathers all around and these gowns were long and trailed behind her.

The house was also furnished in harmony with her. It was overdraped, overcushioned, overcarpeted, overeverything. The walls were blended with the floors by overlapping rugs, bear and tiger skins and portieres. One had to negotiate seven layers of different materials before being able to open a window. There were palms in the corners and at the entrances of rooms and hanging from the ceiling. And there were chandeliers and fishbowls and two canary cages, a parrot and a lapdog. . . . Oh, and several cases with knickknacks and a sea of exotic curiosities, painted shells and bric-a-brac hanging from walls and spread over the piano, little tables and mantels.

All this, however, as well as the mistress of the house, seemed a bit old, tarnished, dusty and patched together. Tia Mariquita and her house gave the impression that they had seen better times. Of course the whole ensemble was old-fashioned, but it was something more than that, it was that feeling of forgotten antiquity of a few years which is more intense than the antiquity of many centuries, and I don't know why one felt that should one move a single piece of furniture there, the whole arrangement would collapse or disappear into thin air. Tia Mariquita often assumed a sad pose and spoke vaguely of her past:

"Those were the times! I remember those receptions, the time I entered and they took me for the Queen of . . . I don't remember what country, but I know that they took me for a queen. Those were the times!"

She referred often to having lost a great deal of money and then I fancied that the row of relatives looked obviously alarmed.

Dr. José de los Rios, who took me there and who knew her rather well and had assisted her in one or two nervous attacks, made an attempt at a diagnosis.

"You know," he said to me, "it is this atmosphere in which she lives. Everything here has remained stagnant, everything here belongs to the day before yesterday and she must refer to it. The windows are always shut and the outside air never comes in. Everything here would probably evaporate if it did. Even Tia Mariquita herself. She could not possibly stand the outside air. It would kill her. I have forbidden her to try it if she wants to keep alive. When she goes out she must do so in an old-fashioned carriage entirely closed and with as many curtains and cushions inside as possible."

"Do you believe it is as bad as that?"

"Absolutely; certain atmospheres can prove deadly. Look at her secretary. The poor fellow suffers from a persistent cough, which has been treated time and again without results. That cough has become entangled in this house and it is impossible to eradicate it. It probably dwelled in this place for who knows how long and he has inherited it. He believes that he gets a different cough each time, but I have persuaded him that it is the same old cough with short intervals during which it takes a vacation and disappears among the draperies and then comes back to him. It is a persistent cough, an ineludible cough that has got hold of this house and of him and has taken root in both. A traditional cough entrapped inside these walls. Everything is so padded here that the cough does not even resound and therefore will never lose its energy. These traditional coughs are common in Spain."

Dr. de los Rios was a strange physician. Listening to him I was often tempted to believe that medicine was almost a science.

Tia Mariquita was reciting something and accompanying it with a waltz played softly on the piano. When she finished amid the general applause she confessed with lowered eyes that the poetry was her own. Then she went on and sang an air from some opera, and interrupting herself with all the abruptness of a true genius, she exclaimed ecstatically to her audience:

"Although literature has always been my passion, music is my weakness, that is why I love operas so."

Someone said something about operas but I was observing Tia Mariquita and did not listen. She answered:

"Oh, yes, I heard Gayarre the divine as they called him, and since then I cannot think of *Il Trovatore* or *Rigoletto* without the tears coming into my eyes. . . . He visited me, we spoke of music, and he told me that he had never met such an understanding person before. He stood there, right where you are."

Everybody looked at a gentleman who had an air of suffering from chronic colic and who was standing by the piano. A pensive expression came into his face to intensify his distressing aspect. Tia Mariquita went on:

"Yes, he stood right there and he sang his famous air 'Spirito Gentile' and I accompanied him. . . . At that time I could play; I am nothing but a shadow of what I was then." And Tia Mariquita went on to explain that when they finished they were both crying like children and he exclaimed in a rapture:

"You are an inspiration, it is a privilege to be accompanied by you. Today I have discovered the true 'Spirito Gentile,' and I shall never sing it with anybody else."

And Tia Mariquita added:

"He was so gallant! Poor Gayarre, he died soon after and never sang it again. Those were the times!"

The gentleman who stood where Gayarre had sung said:

"And do you remember that air from *La Forza del Destino* he used to sing? Trala, lara, lara . . . do you remember it?"

"Of course, I do." Tia Mariquita played something else by some other composer, showing the whites of her eyes while vocalizing and curling her fingers, without paying attention to the puzzled expression on the man's face who could not recognize the air from *La Forza del Destino* and who followed her arpeggios and scales with a twisted mouth. He was about to protest but already everybody was echoing:

"Delightful, delightful . . . !"

And he had to content himself with standing where Gayarre had stood.

After that the chocolate was served and everybody pounced on it with eagerness and resolution. The younger nephews and nieces, however, were held back by a fusillade of parental looks and Tia Mariquita taking a platter went from one to the other giving each a round flat cake and repeating:

"*El bizcocho de la Tia Mariquita.*"

From a distance she looked exactly like a priest delivering communion.

At this moment another person made his presence noticed by a deep cough. It was the secretary of Tia Mariquita, a fellow by the name of Cendreras whose face always looked as if he had just stepped out of a steam bath.

Cendreras shuffled across the carpeted floor without making the slightest noise. He was in slippers and wore a smoking jacket. Without saluting anyone he helped himself to some chocolate and biscuits and mixed in the general conversation as if he had just left the room a minute before, coughing intermittently.

Once when a cough sounded particularly strong, I looked at Cendreras although the cough seemed to come from no particular direction.

"It was not he that time," said Dr. de los Rios. "That was the house coughing."

I turned to Dr. de los Rios.

"Yes," he continued. "All this is absurd. Do you see all these hungry people? They all have been influenced by this environment and this fantastic woman. They do not exist, they are but shadows of her, they are the perfect family as seen from the viewpoint of one of its individuals. Just a shadow, something to give the individual a relative position socially. They are waiting impatiently for her death, for the day when she will shed her identity and her inheritance among them. Then they will live, or at least exist."

I signaled Dr. de los Rios to lower his voice.

"Don't worry, they can't hear. They live on a different plane and do not exist in our world."

In effect he was speaking in a loud voice and yet nobody seemed to hear him and Dr. de los Rios went on talking to me.

From him I gathered that the only person in the whole family with any sense was her husband. He had a good sense of humor, too. He was the only one who had found a practical use for all those draperies and rugs and cushions. When he had money to spare, he changed a bill and then scattered the change all over the house, with the result that when he was out of funds one could always see him down on all fours, looking under a chair or a bed, shaking a portiere here and lifting a cushion there. In that manner he gathered pocket money. According to Dr. de los Rios, he never was much around the house, he was outside and traveling most of the time and that is why he kept his sense.

"He is a curious type," Dr. de los Rios finished. "It is very entertaining to listen to him. He has had an active and adventuresome life. You will like him when you meet him."

"What is his name? Because I only know this lady as Tia Mariquita."

"His name is Olózaga. I have known him for a very long time. As a matter of fact, I knew him long before he married Tia Mariquita."

"Where did you meet him?"

"Long ago, in the Philippine Islands when they were Spanish. I practiced medicine there for the first time. I was quite young then and all I knew was how to administer quinine by the barrel."

"One has to take a lot of that in the colonies, I understand."

"It depends to some degree on whom the colonizer is, and where the colonies are located."

Dr. de los Rios turned the conversation of his own accord upon Olózaga.

According to him, Olózaga was a strong personality, and Tia Mariquita was but one of the fanciful turns of his life. All that family of hers was nothing but a stage setting of wax figures without life of their own, to keep things going while the strange fascination of Olózaga's presence was missing. And Dr. de los Rios added:

"Sometimes when I see all this I fancy him behind the scenes, laughing mockingly. . . . Some people say that he is wicked. I like him. . . . After all, these are nothing but wax figures."

I remembered then that Dr. de los Rios had already spoken once before about Señor Olózaga, when he was going to introduce me to Tia Mariquita. He had said:

"She is a colorful aspect of his life."

By this time the chocolate was finished and Tia Mariquita announced that she was going to read a play of her own composition. Dr. de los Rios excused himself saying that he had to call on a patient and, as I felt rather lost there without him, I decided to go also.

Tia Mariquita saw us to the door talking with Dr. de los Rios about her nerves. In the corridor, where we had to squeeze our way between trinkets and odd furniture, she stopped before a console and assumed a theatrical pose worthy of Sarah Bernhardt.

"This is the grave of my child. There I keep all his little clothes and the things he used before he died and was cast into the eternal sea." She staggered a bit effectively and laid her hands on our shoulders as if we were two supporting characters before a large audience: true Sarah Bernhardt style.

133

"Never mention this to Olózaga." She always addressed him by his second name. "He does not want to be reminded of it. It kills him, it breaks his heart. It has been the tragedy of our lives. It was not our lot to see our heir grow." She pointed again at the console:

"This is a very old piece of furniture. It comes from the Orient and belonged to an ancestor of Olózaga, a Chinese prince whose only daughter also . . ."

"Why, Tia Mariquita," interrupted Dr. de los Rios, "this seems to me a common Spanish *bargueño,* and not at all old; you know, that good varnished Spanish pine. . . ."

Tia Mariquita turned on him indignantly:

"That is nothing but envy, you are always trying to ridicule the most sacred things."

"Don't get mad, Tia Mariquita, you know I always like to tease you."

She turned to me—a decided concession:

"Do not believe him. He is always joking. It is really a very old Oriental work of art."

Although I did not see anything Oriental about it, I nodded respectfully.

In the street Dr. de los Rios asked me:

"Do you know why she insisted that we should not mention that only-child-grave business to Olózaga?"

"Because it grieves him, I suppose."

"Of course not. It is because he does not know anything about it. It is one of the stories she has worked out all by herself. She is as sterile as a mule and could not have a child if she had lain with a bishop."

"And what is that about the Chinese ancestor of her husband?"

"I forgot to tell you. Olózaga seems to have Oriental blood in him of some kind. I don't know whether Chinese or something else. You will see by his features when you meet him. Perhaps that is also imagina tion. He was a bit given to the romantic, too, and I believe he has encouraged her disrespect for truth."

I reminded Dr. de los Rios that he was supposed to call on a patient

"I just said that in order to get away. Didn't you hear her say that she was going to read a play? I could not stay and listen to that thing again."

"Have you heard it already?"

"A thousand times."

"Is it any good?"

"It is ghastly, but she persists in being a playwright."

The Theater

And then I learned that the play in question was what brought about her marriage with Olózaga.

He was in Madrid at that time backing up cheap shows. He met her somehow. She showed him the play and he produced it. The play was so bad that everybody began to speak about it as the worst play they had seen. Everybody went to the theater to have a good time laughing at the play. They called the authoress to the stage and applauded long and cheered and she came out delighted, taking it all as a real tribute to her genius. Perhaps it was in a way. In that manner the house was full every night and they made money. One day Cendreras the secretary told Olózaga that the public was just ridiculing his wife and having a good time at her expense, but Olózaga told him that his wife was happy and they were making money, so why not overlook that trifle?

After that they went into the theater business and toured Spain in vaudeville. Everything was done in the cheapest and most rampant style. They gathered a bunch of starving actors who would perform for next to nothing and went on that way. There were one or two one-act plays in which Tia Mariquita played. The public continued to mock her and applaud and pay. She had a collection of Spanish shawls and every time the public called her she appeared in a different one and the public made it its business to exhaust the supply of shawls, until she appeared again with the same one and then someone would cry: "We have seen that one already." Then she felt insulted and called the public *cochons,* a word she had taken from the French and thought very disdainful. Cendreras told Dr. de los Rios all these things.

One day they were in Bilbao and decided to present her play again. It had been rearranged as a musical comedy with music by a certain

Paroddi, an Italian they had accumulated in their theatrical life. It was a sordid performance. The leading lady had been taken sick and Tia Mariquita had to take her place. They could not find an orchestra cheap enough and they hired a piano out of tune. The singers in their turn were out of tune and out of time with the piano. The settings did not go with the play and shook threateningly. At the end of the second act, half of the settings came down and Tia Mariquita had a fit in the middle of the stage. It was a disastrous performance. The public they met there were not so patient and began to hiss and pound their feet on the floor. Tia Mariquita, who had recovered, became furious at this behavior and showed the audience her middle finger, a vulgar action she had learned from her theatrical crowd and the offensive meaning of which she did not know apparently. This enraged the public, someone threw something at the stage and then the storm broke. The people began to yell and call her all kinds of names. They went out into the street demanding their money back and called out for the drawers of Olózaga. I could never get the meaning of this last demand.

At the stage door they met Olózaga. He discharged a terrible blow at the first one who approached him. At that time he must have been over sixty years old. The mob rushed at him and he smashed right and left and with the poor aid of Cendreras succeeded in holding the mob back until the police came. Poor Cendreras was badly hurt in the fight, but Olózaga did not have a single scratch and was only exhausted. More than sixty years is not the age to face a furious mob.

"And what did they do after that?"

"Well, they quit the theater and settled in Madrid. Since then he has attempted several other business ventures but with little success. He is quite old now, you know, and is beginning to slow down. It is the action of time. No matter how much vitality a man may have, time will get him sooner or later. Everything decays."

We spoke longer about Olózaga and Tia Mariquita and then Dr. de los Rios related to me some of the businesses into which the former had gone.

Business of Señor Olózaga

One day I was sitting at a café in La Plaza de Cataluña in Barcelona. My attention, as well as that of several passersby and people sitting in the café, was attracted by a strange group that was advancing across the plaza.

There were six men dressed in a fantastic manner. They wore jackets with broad green and yellow stripes and also high hats with the same kind of stripes. They were coming toward the café.

When they were nearer, I noticed a man walking in front of them who was doing all he could to shrink within his clothes. He was literally looking for a hole in the ground that would swallow him.

At last the poor fellow dashed across and sat at a table in the café. The six men followed very seriously and sat at a table next to him and remained there silent and motionless. I asked a waiter what it was all about.

"They belong to an agency for the collection of delinquent accounts. It has been working for the last month or so."

The agency worked as follows:

If a person had not paid a debt, the matter was placed in the hands of the agency. Immediately six men dressed in the manner described posted themselves at the door of the victim's house. The moment the debtor came out they followed him closely. If he took a carriage, they took another carriage. If he visited someone, they waited at the door until he came out and then resumed their activities. They followed him everywhere, constantly, until the whole thing became a nightmare. The most stubborn debtor would finally give in to this persecution and, in order to get rid of this pest and public ridicule, pay his debt and be immediately left in peace. No one had been known to last out a week. The agency pocketed part of the debt, and that was the business.

Plainly the man who had sat at the café was ill at ease. He shifted on his chair and turned his back to his tormentors. People were already gathering and pointing at the men and at the debtor, and laughing.

At last the poor man rose. He approached one of the six men and exchanged a few words with him. A carriage was summoned and they all piled inside and went away. On the back of one of the men I saw plainly written in thick letters:

AGENCIA OLOZAGA

The same Olózaga, I thought, always the same imaginative and resourceful spirit, always the same public-arousing love for the colorful, always new and refreshing in his conceptions.

When I left Barcelona I heard that the agency had been dissolved by the police as scandalous, abusive and mob-gathering.

When I went back to Madrid I found Olózaga already established in another business.

The thing consisted of selling the clothes that had belonged to dead people. This idea was not original and, as a matter of fact, it had been worked often in Spain.

When a man dies in Spain (and I suppose anywhere else, for that matter) he is dressed in decent clothes. Whether he is poor or rich he usually has a nice suit of clothes, his Sunday best, generally black, to wear in his coffin. This is the psychology of the business.

The question is to get hold of this suit, and this is the technique: If the family is poor, between having lost its main support and with the expenses which the funeral entails, they are in need of funds and sometimes it is easy to buy the suit cheaply before the coffin is closed. Sometimes the price must be slightly elevated because there is someone in the family whose measurements coincide more or less with those of the deceased. But usually the man who runs the business introduces himself as the representative of some charitable organization. In an eloquent speech he points out that the suit will be used to more advantage covering the nakedness of some poor person than under the ground. That it will be an act of charity that will greatly please the deceased, that it will arouse the gratefulness of the poor on earth and of the Lord in Heaven, and that many prayers will be said for the generous soul of the dead man. Under the circumstances the family usually gives up the suit without investigating further.

However, in difficult cases it is necessary to deal with the grave digger in the cemetery and get him to exercise his pull with the dead

These suits, usually in good condition after a little sponging and pressing, are sold not as secondhand but as misfit, and they leave a good profit. In order to eradicate certain odors which may have clung to them, they are sprayed with a powerful disinfectant, the smell of which has come to be identified with that of death and is most persistent and insidious.

The result is that when an innocent person buys one of these *misfits,* expecting it to pass for a regular suit, he goes by trailing an accusing and funereal atmosphere, which his friends immediately detect with consequent mirth and irreverently sarcastic sallies.

Olózaga had gone into this business associated with a man, Don Laureano Baez, a rogue after whom the police had been for some time.

I met Olózaga one summer's day at the street of Alcala in Madrid. As I saw him coming toward me, outlined against the setting sun, he still looked a big man, but not quite so large as before. He was dressed in a black coat with white flannel trousers, a panama hat, and carried a walking stick. His complexion was fairer now, his eyes were still as oblique and quite puffed underneath. His drooping mustache, as well as his hair, was white and not as long at the ends, and he had quite a heavy abdomen. Europe had softened him as much as Europe could, but there was still that exotic and buoyant air about him.

We had not seen each other for some time and we sat at La Elipa and there he told me about his business.

"Yes," he said. "Everything is decadent now. Even I, who have been so active and resourceful all my life, must content myself with this petty business. In my day, there were adventure and opportunities. Nowadays a man steps out into life and life does not give him a chance to display his ability. The time for opportunities is gone. I have outlived my epoch and that is the worst mistake a man can do. I feel superfluous."

We drank something and talked on, then we walked slowly toward La Castellana.

The Last Glow

A few days after I had seen Olózaga, Madrid was shaken by a crime in which he was involved indirectly. The whole thing came out in the papers, which were full of the accounts.

It seems that Don Laureano Baez, the partner of Olózaga, had a good-looking daughter called Maria Luisa, who was known by the nickname of Lunarito. Olózaga liked the girl and for some time had tried to come to an agreement with Don Laureano whereby the latter would let him have Lunarito for a certain amount of money. They had had several quarrels over this matter and had not been able to come to any agreement. Don Laureano wanted more money.

Then Olózaga began to gamble and win at the Casino de Madrid. He kept this up for several nights and one night when he had been particularly lucky he received a message. It was a letter from Don Laureano Baez saying that he would accept the price they had discussed and to come right away. That he would find the door open and Lunarito waiting for him.

Olózaga communicated immediately with his secretary, Cendreras and sent him to the house of Don Laureano, following at some distance. When he arrived he saw the house of Don Laureano completely dark inside. In the street before the house, someone had built a bonfire and the whole front of the house was illuminated with a red glow.

Olózaga saw Cendreras enter the house. He waited long but Cendreras never came out.

There were several repugnant incidents that leaked out in connection with this crime which it is not necessary to describe. Lunarito was found guilty of murder, as was Don Laureano. He was given life imprisonment at the age of eighty and Lunarito, due to her age and after a long and notorious trial, was sent to a place of correction.

The Spanish public has sometimes romantic and novelistic reactions which are curious in such an old country. The case of Lunarito appealed greatly to the public imagination and several young men of the best society offered to marry and redeem her. A young man about town, by the name of Gaston Bejarano, who enjoyed a certain degree of popularity due to his gay life and the free way in which he spent money, succeeded in marrying her and added thus to his popularity.

I met Olózaga a few days later and he showed me a paper, laughing: "The fool Bejarano," he said, "just like everybody else in his family. I knew his grandfather and he was just as big a fool. You know? It is curious. Every girl or woman I have liked has married well. . . . Five of them married me." He laughed again.

Then he turned to another page in the paper:

"These stupid Frenchmen have just spoiled a good business for me. Here is an article saying that they expect to inundate the Sahara Desert and make a sea out of it. I was just about to organize a company to exploit that desert. A chemist friend of mine told me that there was no cleanser as good as plain sand and I was about to sell the Sahara Desert at ten centimes a box. Another good business spoiled."

"That is very unfortunate," I said.

We walked silently a while. Olózaga said suddenly:

"But now that I think of it, that idea of making a sea out of the desert is really fascinating and offers infinite opportunities. I think I will get hold of a man I know who will give me a few pointers and perhaps I can do something big with it."

A young *modistilla* passed us by. Olózaga, by force of habit, passed her a *piropo* and the girl smiled and winked at him.

Olózaga shook me by the hand:

"Sorry to leave you so soon, but I have important business. So long."

"So long."

And then I thought:

Already in the age of dreams and meaningless pursuits. Same Olózaga and great Chinelato, always after love and adventure and then the paradox . . . by always running after the practical he has lived a most romantic life. His life is a lesson. But now his time is gone. He is right: he has outlived his epoch . . . and that is sad.

The Necrophil

MY TRUE FRIENDSHIP WITH DR. JOSÉ DE LOS RIOS DATES FROM THE time of the incidents I am about to narrate. Although I had met him some time before, it was not until then that I came into close contact with him.

The incidents are as follows:

Doña Micaela Valverde was a middle-aged woman who lived alone with a servant in the Barrio de Salamanca, the same part of Madrid where Dr. José de los Rios had his residence.

Not having any near relatives and to all appearances very little interest in life, Doña Micaela concentrated her activities to a great degree on going to church. She went to early Mass at dawn, to the benediction in the evening, and during the middle part of the day she always engaged in some sort of novena, or else in one of those cumulative series of prayers in which one prays one paternoster the first day, two paternosters the second and so on, up to fifty or whatever the top number may be, and then decreases the dose accordingly, just as one does with medicines which are dosified, by increasing and decreasing the number of drops.

With these dosified prayers one is supposed to attain practically any purpose which comes under the dominion of the saint to which they are dedicated, or the saint may even be moved by such perseverance to use his influence with bigger saints or with God himself.

These cumulative demands upon heaven were a specialty with Doña Micaela, but I have been unable to discover what she could demand so persistently and constantly.

Doña Micaela Valverde was just as the reader will imagine her, but with the exception that she was not lean. Of course, her features and expression were hard and she was pale, but she was not lean and, as a matter of fact, she was rather well developed. If it had not been for her perennial black attire and something more difficult to define about her, she would have come under the adjective of attractive.

However, there was something about Doña Micaela that was weird. Dr. José de los Rios called my attention to this fact. It was that appearance of a wax figure that no matter how faithful an imitation it may be of nature, is always sordid. Her clothes did not wrap Doña Micaela with a warm, soft caress as they do other people; they just lay on her with apprehension and coldness, visibly displeased by the close contact. Those clothes did not cover a resilient flesh that yields and adapts itself to its surroundings, they seemed to cover a stiff frame and that reluctantly as one who complies with a distasteful duty. Seeing Doña Micaela one realized that clothes sometimes have feelings.

Aside from her churchgoing, Doña Micaela had another hobby and this was to attend funerals. She just loved them and was present at every funeral she could gain access to. As her acquaintances could not furnish her with enough material to satisfy her voracity, she was known to chase all over Madrid looking at doors and windows, and wherever she discovered the slightest sign of death she rushed in and, under any pretext, literally forced her presence upon the grief-stricken gathering, often saying that she had known the deceased at some time. She uttered indelicate and tactless comments, gloating over the most repugnant details.

She would say, devouring the corpse with her eyes:

"How thin he looks! He must have suffered greatly."

"Why, no, Doña Micaela, he had a very pleasant death, fortunately, just as if he had gone to sleep."

"Hmm . . . his features look distorted to me. His agony must have been long. . . . Hmm . . . yes, this is terrible. I remember my poor

Joaquin . . . yes. It was apoplexy and he was all black in the face. . . .
Hmm. . . . It was horrible. . . . I was like a madwoman and wouldn't let
them take him away. . . . Hmm . . . until the neighbors complained
because of the smell. . . . Hmm. . . . It was great. . . . Hmm. . . . I mean,
terrible."

Doña Micaela gave the corpse a last long look and even stroked it if
no one was looking, and then rushed to another funeral, leaving the
family in a worse condition than before.

She entered the next place with a professional air.

"Hmm . . . we have death today, I perceive. I am Doña Micaela
Valverde, at your service. Hmm . . . you did not know me, but I was a
good friend of hers. . . . Yes, this is terrible."

"It is very kind of you, Señora Valverde, to show this last attention. . . ."

"Tut tut, my child, it is a pleasure. . . . Hmm. . . . I assure you it is a
pleasure."

Doña Micaela turned several times about the bed or coffin, as the
case might be, with a critical air, looking, sniffing, if possible touching.

"Did you stuff all her cavities carefully, my child? Hmm . . . you had
better let me adjust that serviette about her face, it is loose and her
mouth is not completely closed. . . . Hmm . . . she looks like a person
with a toothache and not like a regular corpse." And Doña Micaela
proceeded to adjust the napkin with nimble, pale hands that matched
the corpse, delaying the operation, handling the body as much as
possible and talking all the time:

"I remember the time that my poor Nicolas died. . . . I forgot to close
his mouth and when they carried him away it was wide open . . . as if
he were still yelling from the pains he had before he died. . . . Hmm . . .
these things are terrible. . . . I shall never forget those moments at the
cemetery when they buried my two poor husbands. . . . Hmm. . . . I can
still hear the sound of the first pail of dirt upon the coffin."

And then Doña Micaela rushed away.

"Good-by, my child, and don't forget to call me the next time."

When Doña Micaela arrived home she was all out of breath.

"Jacinta," she addressed her old maid, "five funerals today. Hmm . . .

very good day . . . yes. I have not wasted my time."

Jacinta shook her head and went back to her kitchen silently.

At night Doña Micaela frequented the *tertulia* of an undertaker down the street, and there she spoke of death to her heart's content and argued long with her host. She could not bring him around to see things in her way. The undertaker liked death in a philosophical manner. He regarded it as a business question, whereas Doña Micaela considered it purely from an aesthetic viewpoint. She liked death for itself. However, they both agreed upon one thing: that there were not as many deaths as they would have liked, and they often held conversations like this:

"I don't know what is the matter this winter. It does not seem to get cold enough."

"No. I have not heard yet of a single case of pneumonia, not even a bad cold."

"Yes . . . it is terrible. They speak so much about that famous breeze from the Guadarrama. . . . Hmm. . . . I have not seen it do any harm yet.'

"And with so many old people in Madrid, too! All they need is a little cold wind and . . ."

"Yes. . . . Hmm . . . very discouraging. . . . I mean. . . . Hmm . . . yes.'

Doña Micaela and the undertaker were good friends. She helped him in his business and he helped her in her hobby. She had become a most accomplished sleuth for death. She could scent it a mile away. She often said that she could see in people's faces if they were going to die soon and she often communicated these hunches to her friend the undertaker and he made his preparations.

On the other hand, he allowed her to potter around his funeral paraphernalia and she had even seen him work on several occasions. Of course, they did not admit openly their mutual weakness, but they knew that they could count on each other's sympathy. They spoke of their pet subject in an unctuous voice verging on obscenity:

"You know Garcia, the poet across the street from my house? Well, I know he is going to die soon. I never liked him . . . always reciting his secondhand poems about life and nature to everyone. . . . Hmm . . . he is already blind and I know he will die. . . . Hmm. . . . I could see the sign of agony in his face. And it is that girl, Lunarito, who lives with him. . . . Hmm . . . yes, she is killing him . . . she is a beast. . . . Hmm . . . and those two big gloomy dogs he keeps, like reincarnations of souls in pain. . . . Hmm . . . yes. They have been howling at night. . . . Hmm. . . ."

Doña Micaela loved death. It was an obsession with her that had assumed indecent proportions. She spoke of nothing else, she thought of nothing else, and people began to notice it subconsciously. She always appeared as if by miracle on the spot and everyone began to fear her presence. There was that wax figure air about her, that cloud of horror that seemed to hang about her person. There was that deep look in her eyes that seemed to search for the corpse in everyone she met, that looked for the death that is latent in every living being. That drilling look of hers that penetrated the skin and caressed the skull, that boring look that reminded everyone she saw of the fact that his days were counted. That look which enclosed one like a shroud.

She also walked in a jerky manner as if she were a stiff, mechanical dummy. With her black clothes at night, in a lonely, dark street, she must have been more than enough to frighten the most courageous person, and streets were lonely and dark then in the Barrio de Salamanca.

And then I found out another important thing about Doña Micaela Valverde.

She suffered from a strange sickness. Once every year and for the space of two or three months she went into a state of unconsciousness which had all the aspects of death. It was something like catalepsy but more acute. She grew cold and rigid and all efforts to bring her to were vain.

In the beginning these spells were not so acute and she could hear and feel although she could not move or speak. But with time they grew worse and she lay exactly as if she were dead. Her features grew sharper and set into a cadaverous expression, and when she woke up she could remember nothing at all.

By and by she was able to detect the approach of these spells every year and then she went to say farewell to the few acquaintances she had kept, as if she were going for a vacation to the other world. By and by these tours to her friends became a ritual which took place every year about the same time: the spring. And then she retired to her chamber and her house was closed and she lay dead to the world.

Dr. José de los Rios, who attended her more or less, said to me one day:

"Her case interests me and I would like to know more about it, but she won't tell me. I believe she enjoys her condition. She likes to die periodically and I do not think she really wants me to cure her. She innocently believes that we physicians are enemies of death. I know that she dislikes me decidedly, but it amuses me to treat her and threaten her with life. It is surprising how she hates life. She has the same repugnance for life that most people have for death. I mean a repugnance for the obvious manifestations of it, not exempt from slight curiosity. She feels as revolted by the presence of a healthy-looking person as a normal being is by the proximity of a decayed corpse. She hates life."

Doña Micaela Valverde had told little about herself to Dr. de los Rios. However, she had told him that she sensed the approach of her attacks by the long spells of melancholia that preceded them. For almost a month before one of these attacks she felt a sadness which assumed maddening proportions and almost verged on insanity. Then, as the attack neared, cramps began to steal all over her body at regular intervals and she knew it was time to make her preparations.

As I have said, in the beginning these attacks were milder; she lay motionless but her eyelids quivered and sometimes tears rolled from her eyes. She could see, hear and smell and sometimes even feel. But with time these attacks became more severe. She lost consciousness, was seized by complete rigor mortis, her temperature decreased until she was cold and the most sensitive stethoscope could not detect the beating of her heart. In that manner she lay for two or three months in her bed, in a room where the curtains had been drawn, having told her elderly maid beforehand not to give her any attention.

The poor maid went about the house with supreme indifference. She had apparently become used to these things. She arranged things, put everything in order without even looking into her mistress's room, and thus time went by, until one day Doña Micaela would wake up and stagger out of bed hardly able to walk. Then the old maid would see the door of her mistress's room open and Doña Micaela come reeling down the corridor like a living corpse, mumbling in a hollow voice:

"I have been dead.... I have been dead...."

The maid shook her head sadly and went about her duties.

Dr. José de los Rios had examined Doña Micaela during one of her attacks and had said to me:

"I have made all the tests that science knows of for such cases, and I tell you that she is really dead. She dies for two or three months and then she is resuscitated."

"But that is not possible. It must be an acute attack of catalepsy or something like that."

"I have made all the tests and I tell you that she is really dead."

Dr. de los Rios insisted, but I could not be convinced.

Soon there was a superstition about Doña Micaela Valverde, and people began to call her the dead woman. No one dared approach her. Everybody avoided her. Children ran away from her, frightened. The only people who continued to befriend her were her old maid and the undertaker down the street.

Doña Micaela had foreseen the danger of being buried during one of her attacks and she had told her maid not to consent to such a thing until it was absolutely necessary, and under no circumstances to allow the undertaker or anyone who called himself a relative to come to the house during the spell. She seemed to know almost as much about the living as she knew about the dead.

And Doña Micaela went about lonely. She left her house at dusk and walked along the outskirts of the city, seized by infinite sadness and melancholia, and then she wandered in the direction of the church and spent a long time there in a dark corner, praying. Her sadness became more persistent and she went by with bowed head. She cried often and she cried more when she saw people receding from her.

Everyone had left her, everyone fled from the dense atmosphere of death which wrapped her, and when I saw her at that time I fancied that during these periods of her life her features had softened and there was more of a human expression in her face.

However, the repeated visits of death had branded her. Death had left with his deep footprints an indelible mark upon her whole countenance. Her complexion had assumed a greenish hue, her eyes were sunken and surrounded by black shadows, and as she passed by she left a trail of that peculiar odor which was not precisely unpleasant. It was a slightly rancid odor with a strong suggestion of withered orange blossoms and it hit one's nostrils with a thud.

And then there was that look in her great sunken eyes, that look that searched for death in everyone she met. But now that look, too, had been softened, it no longer had that former spark of mockery, it was only a long, sad look, often veiled by tears.

Yes. There was a profound hidden beauty in Doña Micaela, and she might have been an intensely attractive woman. As a matter of fact, she had been married three times. Her two first husbands died and the third one, called Cendreras, left her during one of her death spells.

Dr. de los Rios, who knew Cendreras, told me that he left him the following message for her:

"Tell her that I had to leave her because I felt insanity close upon me.

"Tell her that I loved her more than anything in the world but that love is life and everything with her is death.

"Tell her that every time I saw her coming down that lonely corridor in the house, I felt the chill of fear in my marrow.

"Tell her that she was beautiful but that every time she embraced me I felt as if my grave were closing upon me.

"Tell her that our marriage was never consummated, that in the most intimate moments at night, whenever I approached her, I saw the jealous hands of her dead husbands rising from a black abyss to defend her from me.

"Tell her that in those moments her eyes were the most beautiful I have seen, but that they sent me away by their unearthly expression. That I knew that my intentions were sacrilegious. . . . There was such a mixture of mockery and sadness in those eyes. . . .! As if they were reminding me that she did not belong to this world. And perhaps that saved me from a complete union with death.

"Tell her that during her death spells I roamed about the house like a madman, that it was like living with a corpse, and that every time she came back to life, if I made an effort to address her cheerfully because of her recovery, she looked at me with that expression of mockery and sadness as if saying: *Do not forget yourself, because some day you will be stiff and dead.*

"Tell her that every time she looked at me, I saw myself dead in her eyes.

"Tell her that I left her while she was dead because otherwise she would have held me with her strange fascination.

"Tell her that I fled from that house of death never to return, but that I shall never love another. That she has awakened in me the germ of death which is dormant in every living being.

"And tell her that I will see to it, that when I die my corpse shall be sent to her."

And then Dr. de los Rios said to me:

"Everything about that woman is dead and anyone living with her would die soon. Death is a contagious disease that kills. With her it has become endemic and periodic. She dies often but death cannot kill her completely. There is no better antidote for death than death itself. Anyone about her would have died."

"But then what about her old maid? She lives."

"She is too old, she is no longer emotional, she is past the danger point. Yes, she is too old; death has missed her. Like most old people she will not die, she will just fade away."

"And yet, doctor, Doña Micaela married three times. After all, that is a sign of life. Marriage, I understand, is the consecration of an act of nature, of life, of love."

"I don't know about that. Most things are consecrated after they are dead and perhaps she felt that. She felt that marriage killed that thing which is one of the clearest symbols of life. Three men yielded to her attraction in spite of that something about her that kept everyone from her; and to the three of them she put the same condition of marriage, the same death condition. Two of them paid with their lives and

Cendreras only deferred his payment. He died not long after, the victim of a gruesome murder; but his body could not be sent back to Doña Micaela, as he had promised, because only part of it was found and this in installments, and besides the law objected."

"But was she in love with her husbands?"

"I don't think so. What she loved in them was their corpses. She was in love with Death and I think she sacrificed them as a tribute to him. You know? I do not think she ever consummated any of her marriages. I gathered that from her third husband. She was always true to death."

And one day Dr. José de los Rios took me to the house of Doña Micaela Valverde, who was under one of her death spells.

When we arrived the maid received us. She greeted Dr. de los Rios with affability and said:

"There she is in her room, dead. You know where her room is."

There was great indifference in her gesture and her sentence rang with a broad, tragic humor in the lonely house.

We advanced through a corridor illuminated by a window at one end which projected our shadows in our path. We advanced, pushing our shadows ahead until they met the opposite wall and began to creep upward. They rose menacingly before us, but, as we approached them, they shrank. At the end of that corridor was the chamber of Doña Micaela Valverde.

The room was quite dark. I saw faintly the outline of her body upon the bed. Dr. de los Rios circled around her and threw the curtains aside. The room was illuminated by the yellow light of the late afternoon. It was quite dismantled, with scarcely any furniture and this covered with dust. The empty walls were dirty and showed cracks in several places. There was also a thick layer of dust covering the glass of the window, which was closed. This made the yellowish light fainter and colder.

Doña Micaela lay in her bed completely covered, head and all. Dr. de los Rios threw the sheet aside and exposed the dead woman. We both looked at her for a long time. Her eyes were open and in them the frost of death was evident, but they held that strange, deep beauty which characterized them and were surrounded by dark circles leading toward her temples, where they were lost in her hair which lay dry and ashen on the pillow.

On the wall at the head of her bed there was an ivory crucifix upon a black cross, bending over the dead woman with infinite clemency. Dr. de los Rios remarked:

"Her servant forgot to close her eyes this time."

"They are beautiful," I said.

And Dr. de los Rios repeated:

"Yes, they are beautiful."

I remained silent, studying her naked body. Then Dr. de los Rios spoke again:

"I tell you, this is death and nothing else. This woman has been dead a month and will probably be dead for two more."

And he gazed wistfully upon the dead woman and recited in a melancholy voice:

"The ominous thunder will storm the distance only to die unheard in the faint tremor of her eardrums.

"The scorching sun will surmount the meridian over her in silence, without extracting a single responsive drop of sweat, to congeal upon the glaciers of her eyes.

"The dazzling stars of the nights will be put out as they drop like gouts of light in the absolute emptiness left by her soul.

"The blood-red dawn of the days will pale and fade upon her livid corpse.

"And the brilliant cavalcade of happiness will grow quiet when passing her and disperse in listless futility under the great dense pall of her negation."

And then Dr. de los Rios produced a bistoury and with brutal resolution inflicted a deep wound in her thigh.

"Look!" he said and showed me the frozen wound without a drop of blood.

"Touch!" he said, and pressed my reluctant hand against her ice-cold flesh. I withdrew it quickly as another sad scene flashed through my memory, and then looked at the crucifix whose head hung with graceful resignation.

155

Dr. de los Rios continued:

"These are not absolute proofs, but they are the emotional tests for the layman. I have taken the scientific tests and I tell you that she is dead. When she revives, she will have no memory of her condition, all sense of time will be lost. She will think that she went to sleep a moment ago, but she will have vague feelings of what has taken place, a feeling that is unmistakable. She will sense the grip of death all over her like an echo. She is a specialist and she can tell. She will say that she has been dead and she will be right."

"But this is absurd!" I exclaimed. "If she has been dead a month, how is it that putrefaction has not set in?"

My sentence seemed to last very long. Everything in that room appeared to be in a state of suspended animation. We were standing at opposite sides of the bed; Dr. de los Rios had his back to the window and I could only see his outline against the dim light. Evening was coming on fast and the last light was concentrated upon the ivory crucifix and the dead body that lay between us. My sentence was still hanging in the air as if unable to penetrate the death wall that separated us. Dr. de los Rios rose slowly, his outline growing into immense proportions that frightened me. The bistoury glittered in his hand among the gathering shadows like the last light of wisdom trying to pierce the darkness of mystery, endeavoring to reach and dissect the beyond. And then he answered:

"Because putrefaction is the return to life. It is then that life snatches a body from death and claims it as its own. This woman loves death too much. She loves death for itself and has detached it from all the intimate links that bind it to life. Through decomposition a body returns to life, having lost its identity and personality. She wants to remain herself so that when she revives she will know that she has been dead. She only wants the decorative and ephemeral part of death. She regards death only in its purest sense, separated from all its usual and necessary developments within nature. That is why putrefaction does not begin in her. It is too obvious a sign of life and she hates life. But how she can arrest death, how her will can hold good past the boundaries of her life is beyond me."

And Dr. José de los Rios seemed to rise farther, his arm reaching for an invisible fleeting truth. And then the light went out in his bistoury and we were submerged in thick shadows. All I remember then is that Dr. de los Rios took me by the arm and we rushed through the darkness and out of that house of death into the street.

I never knew whether my experiences of that day were a dream or reality. I was busy all that summer and did not see Dr. de los Rios again until the fall. When I saw him I referred to the subject.

"I was finally able to diagnose her case more clearly," he said. "You know? Doña Micaela Valverde was in love with death as I often said. Of course, almost everybody has an interest in death, just as they have an interest in sex. It is the natural curiosity for the beginning and end of existence which affects them very directly. But this interest had grown in Doña Micaela to a love and a passion. She spoke and thought of nothing else."

And then I learned from Dr. de los Rios that she used to visit the morgue and spend hours there at a time and also took lengthy walks in the cemetery.

She finally discontinued her visits to the morgue, because she was afraid to have her weakness detected. Besides, she preferred funerals, where death had its decorative aspects. It was a real passion with her. She liked everything that had a suggestion of death. She liked dummies and collected mannequins and all kinds of dolls. In fact everything wherein she could detect a symbol. Doña Micaela was madly in love with death. Those death spells she suffered were, according to Dr. de los Rios, the little trips she took to join Death and celebrate her nuptials with him. And Dr. de los Rios finished:

"I came to the conclusion that Doña Micaela Valverde was pregnant with death and that the only cure would be to bring about an abortion."

By the time Dr. de los Rios arrived at this conclusion, Doña Micaela was already in bad shape. She was paralyzed and her spells were now more frequent. She spent more of her time dead than alive and death had got a terrible hold on her.

And Dr. de los Rios said:

"Then poor Doña Micaela called me for a consultation. I already knew what medicine she needed. You know how I believe in suicide as a universal panacea. Well, suicide is also an abortion of death."

Therefore, after she told Dr. de los Rios all her troubles, he said that he could not cure her, that her case was hopeless and that the best thing she could do was to commit suicide. That death was the best antidote for death. Death would not come to look for her unless she went to look for him. Her reactions were most surprising. That woman who had died so many times had now developed a tremendous love for life, and the prospect of a temporary death, let alone a permanent one as Dr. de los Rios proposed, made her really furious. She insulted him and said that he did not know his business, that he did not like her and did not want to cure her.

Dr. de los Rios was relentless. He spoke of suicide as eloquently and convincingly as one who does not practice it, and went away leaving in her mantle a gun loaded with blank cartridges.

"And did the trick work?" I asked Dr. de los Rios.

"Perfectly," he answered.

It seems that she became so maddened by the approach of death, which she could sense, that in a moment of strength she decided to kill herself. When she shot off the gun, she fainted but under the effect of a pail of water that her maid emptied on her head, she came to feeling very well. She got out of the chair where she had been confined and walked as if nothing had happened.

And Doña Micaela Valverde is quite all right now. Dr. de los Rios had all her collections of dolls, mummies and mannequins thrown away, told her to move to a cheerful house and forbade her to step into a church again.

Dr. de los Rios says:

"You know? This religious business deals too much with the beyond and creates an obsession of death. There are many cases in Spain like the one of Doña Micaela Valverde. Have you noticed those rows of fanatics dressed in black clothes and looking like corpses that go to the benediction at dusk? Well, every one of them has a more or less marked tendency to necrophilia. Of course, the case of Doña Micaela was acute and verged on obscenity. She was already pregnant with death, but there are many others who, although they do not go so far, often flirt with the idea and one of these days are going to get caught."

"It really was quite an extraordinary case."

"And it had also its romantic touches. Doña Micaela, drawn away from life by her passion, to join her lover in the lonely paths of nothingness. After all, not everything in love is obscene."

"And you say that she is all right now?"

A Romance of Dogs

I

Students

AFTER THE DEATH OF MY FRIEND GARCIA, DR. JOSÉ DE LOS RIOS, WHO had attended him in his last moments, brought me this manuscript which forms part of a kind of self-study Garcia had been composing during his life.

Dr. de los Rios told me that he thought the manuscript would interest me, as it dealt precisely with the time when Garcia and I were schoolfellows and he mentions my name in it.

Aside from the personal interest that this narrative holds for me as a document of my early friendship with Garcia, and the vivid recollections it brings of that period of our lives, I consider that it finds an adequate place in this book and, therefore, am taking the liberty of introducing it here.

This manuscript is perhaps a bit disorderly, obscure or even incoherent, but its deep sincerity renders it, I believe, worthy of a tolerant reading.

CHAPTER

All my memories around the age of ten are wrapped in a cloud resembling those heavenly clouds in the saints' pictures which I used

163

to be given and which I always put aside carefully with a dry and taste-less feeling of duty. All these memories are sprinkled with sadistic scenes portrayed in the pictures: A woman with her heart pierced by many arrows, a man on a cross, bleeding, with a crown of thorns on his head, and a celluloid picture with only a heart aflame.

There are many other pictures which I cannot clearly see, but these three stand out of the fog which surrounds my memories, they stand out as clearly as a man and a woman whom I also remember at that period and a subtle romantic feeling about their lives which either my childish intuition disclosed or my childish imagination fancied to be intimately blended with them.

Why my recollections of that period are so confused must not be held against my memory. I flatter myself at having developed a good ability to remember things and as a matter of fact I remember with amazing precision, as will be seen by the earlier parts of this auto-biography, things which took place long before the ones I am about to narrate. But as I look back now, I know that I neither suffered at that time from an attack of amnesia, nor of stupidity. I simply was sleepy.

Yes, around the age of ten, I was terribly sleepy. I remember the things that happened then as one remembers things that happen when one is half awake. And indeed it was in that general drowsiness that many things began to wake in me, that I was lulled into greater sleepi-ness by the rocking waves of contrary streams of sentiments and emotions, of a great confusion of matters which I did not understand but suspected and into which I went with sleepy curiosity and drowsy fear.

When I was ten or twelve, I am not even sure which, my family moved to Vizcaitia, a village in North Spain where they had been in the habit of spending summers, and I became a student at the Colegio de los Padres Salesianos. I still remember the first impression I received upon arriving at Vizcaitia then. Even at that age I was conscious of the fact that the village had grown smaller since the last time I saw it. Soon after, an existence of hardship and suffering began for me.

Although as a child I had never been particularly fond of Vizcaitia, where I always felt like a stranger unable to mix completely with the other children who spoke *Vascuence,* a dialect which I was always loath to learn, I had always enjoyed there a life of freedom and a certain amount of play and solace. Now I had come to Vizcaitia to live and study, rather to study than to live.

I remember the period that follows, wrapped in a cloud of confusion and horror, which even to this day has left in me a decided feeling of hatred against everything that has to do with schools or study, and perhaps many other feelings into whose description this is not the place to enter.

I was not an intern. I lived with my family and there was a good two kilometers' walk from my house to the school which I had to take twice a day, at seven in the morning and at nine o'clock at night.

The time between these two walks was filled with study, recitations, mental strain, discipline, punishment, fear. . . . And then to walk home at night with a leaden heart and an eighty-page assignment of history for the next day. To study at home, to poison the few moments of freedom for which I had longed all day away from that scholastic prison, amidst the warmth of my family and the tolerance of my parents so different from the cruel strictness of those priests.

And as if that whole day had not been enough to shake my nerves, that walk home was the last bitter and fearful experience of the day. In order to get home I had to pass through a certain street and in that narrow, lonely, dark street there was a big dog, a dog which seemed to have made it his business to frighten me, to bark and to attack me. And I recall taking a long detour in order to avoid the dog or, standing cold and sleepy in the rain, waiting for the horrible animal to go away, and then I remember the confused thoughts that swarmed through my brain.

I had heard the priests repeat time and again that it was necessary to suffer in order to obtain happiness and also say that the devil likes to make us suffer in order to test our faith in Providence. All these things the priests said at the school and many other things which I did not understand very well. Even at that age I was faintly aware of the absurdity of such a tragic and self-punishing attitude about life. However, there was this dog. This dog was standing between me and the home and family which made me happy, and as his shadow loomed before me and as I stood there or circled around the village the priests' words came back to me. There was a confusion of unpleasant experience and persistent teaching and that dog became for me the symbol of suffering before attaining happiness. That dog was there to test me or to tempt me. I did not know which, and I do not know to this day whether I thought the dog was God or the devil.

But I know one thing: that the dog became for me a nightmare, an enemy. It was an object of constant fear and this, together with the fact that my nervous system was weak due to lack of sleep and overwork, formed an obsession which haunted me day and night.

I left school at night and arrived home late. I had no appetite to eat my dinner and rushed through it in order to prepare my homework. Homework after fourteen hours spent in school. Every night as my mother pressed me to eat and asked me about school, I felt the same mad desire to cry and tell her to take me away from it all, but the idea of duty, study and sacrifice had been impressed on my young brain by that constant preaching and teaching always mixed with religious and mystic doctrines. I was too young to weigh matters freely in my mind. I was terribly tired and everything was confused. I only knew that there was duty, that I had to study, and even at that age I felt that should I speak, they would not understand, just as I did not understand them when they spoke.

I did not say what I wanted and that made things worse. I answered my mother that everything was all right and then began to study, my tired brain making a useless effort to memorize as we were told to, word by word, comma by comma, lessons written in a language too abstruse for any child, rhetorical and florid passages filled with empty words whose meaning no young person could understand, and I kept at this with fear in my heart until I fell asleep at midnight. Then my mother took the books and papers from under my head and said: *no estudies mas* but I could not hear her. I kept at it every night and I kept at it in vain.

On winter mornings, at five o'clock when it was still dark, I remember the maid coming into the room with half-shut eyes carrying a cup of black coffee:

"Señorito, señorito, despiertese."

And I sat up and drank the coffee and she went back to sleep. And then I took the books from my bed (I even slept with books) and began again to study or rather to make myself believe that I was studying by looking blankly at the books and turning over the leaves.

For me duty had become a series of meaningless and mechanical motions and as long as I went through them, my conscience felt relieved, but underneath there was fear.

Then to dress and swallow the hateful breakfast and to rush away to school in order to be there at seven-thirty in time for Mass. That daily Mass, that perennial Mass, that unfailing and persistent Mass in a dark chapel and in obscure Latin. Such a drowsy ritual and such drowsy language after having had only five hours' sleep. And another day.

That is why I say that at the age of ten I was terribly sleepy and everything in my memory seems to grow dim as if in a daze. A mixture of fog and fear, of suffering and misunderstanding.

I remember few pleasant things at that time, but I want to mention them. One of these was what we called Los Madrileños, a group formed by the few boys in that school who came from Madrid.

The Basque Provinces for some reason or other entertain a grudge against Madrid and all its products. In the Basque Provinces, or at least in Vizcaitia, they call people from Madrid *Maquetos,* a name which I believe is insulting and implies something like ill-born. That is what the other boys called us at school: *El Círculo de los Maquetos* (The Club of the Ill-born) and we were naturally thrown together by this general animosity and faithfully stuck to each other. After the recitations, while the other boys spoke *Vascuence* we spoke Spanish and were proud of it. We also sat together in the study hall.

Los Madrileños formed a very small group. We were only four: Julio Cavañas (we always called him Cavañitas), Pepe Bejarano, Felipe Alfau and myself.

Another pleasant thing was Padre Inocencio. Although he was a Basque, born in Bilbao, he had lived a long time in Madrid where he had many friends and still went there often for short trips. We naturally felt that he sympathized with our cause and he lent us moral support.

As I have already said, everything at that period is vague in my mind, but I know that he held some important post, a director, chaplain or something at a convent that was located on the same road, next door to our school. When he was in Vizcaitia, he always spent part of the day in our school where he taught literature and part of the day at the convent, I presume attending to whatever duties he might have had there. To be very frank, I do not know whether there are chaplains or directors at convents, for, as I have overlooked saying, my ignorance about all matters which constituted my daily routine at that time is appalling. It is easy to understand considering the condition of my mind during those days. But at any rate I know that Padre Inocencio was connected with the convent in some important capacity.

Padre Inocencio was somewhat of an exception and a revolutionary character in the village and among the other priests. He was a good friend of my family and a constant member of our home gatherings while we stayed at Vizcaitia.

All these circumstances made me feel that I had a friend and protector while he was at the school. I grew rather fond of Padre Inocencio and Mother liked him very well, a thing which made him grow still more exceptional in my eyes, since it was not a secret at home, not even to me then, that she had a decided contempt for anything connected with the Church. The only reason why my mother ever let me attend a school of priests is because it was the only so-called good school in Vizcaitia, because practically all reliable schools in Spain are in the hands of priests or nuns and because one seldom finds a school in Spain where something pertaining to the Church is not hidden in some corner. Perhaps Padre Inocencio had a hand in it also.

But as I was saying, my mother liked Padre Inocencio and in the attempt to describe his character partly, I am quoting her.

Padre Inocencio was a worldly person. He liked society and the arts. He was an accomplished landscape painter and a good poet. His all-around culture and fine graceful manners set him high above the general rabble of Spanish priests whose rampant and sordid ways are most obnoxious, and who literally steal their way into the homes and pockets of really good people by craftiness and the well-combined use of superstition and fear of hell.

Padre Inocencio did not mix much with the other priests. In the afternoons while the roads of Vizcaitia swarmed with gentlemen of the frock from all the nearby monasteries, in their dark robes, like an army of cockroaches, Padre Inocencio could be seen walking alone through some hidden pathway reading his book of prayers, perhaps dreaming, cleanly shaven, subdued, unobtrusive, a decided contrast to the other priests.

And yet Padre Inocencio was not a born ascetic. I have heard Mother say so. And it was all he could do to keep mundane thoughts away and to conquer the stubborn flesh. Padre Inocencio was a born romantic and he loved the world too much. He had taken orders, and although it was more than he could bear, he would rather curb his feelings than sacrifice a promise he had made openly and accepted of his own accord, and he was constantly disentangling himself from the snares set in his pathway by the seven mortal sins, as my mother used to put it.

Padre Inocencio suffered a constant internal warfare. He liked women as much as women liked him. His engaging personality had won him the favor of all the ladies in Vizcaitia and they would either confess their sins to no one else, or confess to anyone but him.

But much as Padre Inocencio was tempted, he never yielded and I have heard Mother say that he was the only priest she had known to lead a chaste and ascetic life in Spain.

And such was his character to the best of my knowledge:

Padre Inocencio was an exceptional priest.

He never stole.

He never prevaricated.

He never committed rape.

He always sacrificed himself.

And one day he committed suicide.

Why Padre Inocencio took his own life is more or less of a mystery to all those who knew him. To me it is fatality. Everything that took place at that time was imprinted on my mind through such a cloud of confusion that it sweeps my memory like a hurricane of disconnected phenomena, apparently without cause or effect.

Some people say, among them my mother, that the vows were too much of a burden for him and that he realized he was incapable of going through with the life of a priest. Some other people say that there was an unhappy love affair, that his vows rose between him and his love and that he decided to destroy himself before destroying his vows. It seems to me that both explanations come down to the same thing. I have no personal opinion upon the subject. I will simply attempt to extricate from the fog surrounding them the few outstanding happenings in my memory which preceded this unhappy ending.

One day we learned that Padre Inocencio was going to Madrid and, what is worse, that he was taking Pepe Bejarano back to his family, who were going to send him to school in England.

Padre Inocencio interceded in our favor and we Los Madrileños were given permission to accompany them to the station.

Not one of us spoke during the ride. We, the ones who were to be left behind, felt a mixture of sadness and admiration for our lucky companion.

For some reason or other we felt that to speak to Pepe at this moment was to take too many liberties with an important person. An embarrassing barrier of formality had suddenly sprung up between us who had always been so intimate. We were all silent and even Padre Inocencio only spoke a few necessary words. At that time I flattered myself that he must have felt sad to part with us. Now I know how little important we must have appeared to him, with our fallen socks, our dirty school robes and our dusty *boinas.*

As they boarded the train, there was some effusiveness. Pepe set the example; he embraced Cavañitas and then each one of us. Padre Inocencio patted us on the cheek and placed a conical package of sweets in Alfau's hands:

"For all of you, and don't fight for them. Now run along to school and be good boys."

As the train departed, Pepe shouted from the window:

"*Sostened el nombre de los Madrileños.*"

Blushing and feeling quite silly, we all answered in chorus that we would and there we remained for a while watching the train recede.

Then there comes another fog in my memory out of which only one incident stands out clearly like a colorful picture upon a black background.

I cannot recall the circumstances or even how it came about. I only remember that I was standing with my mother in the road that led to the school and that she was talking to a man who held a horse by the bridle.

Then the man helped my mother on the horse and she drove away as far as the school and then turned back at full gait.

My mother was very blond and was dressed in some sort of green dress. The sun was bright and the horse big and white.

I remember that my mother's hair came undone and flamed in the wind like molten gold, and that when I saw her approaching thus, upon that great white horse at full gallop, I instinctively shrank back and hung on to the man's coat in a mixture of fear and admiration. I always remember with amazing clearness that dazzling scene, of my mother advancing ominously upon that white horse. I don't know why, but from that day I stopped taking her for granted.

As a contrast to that vivid experience, I do not remember what came after but I knew that there followed a period of studying under the insufferable circumstances of which I have already spoken. I never heard again from Pepe Bejarano. Soon after that, the term ended and the summer holiday began.

But before going on with my narrative, I must tell of an incident which, if I am to trust my confused memories of that time, began and developed during Padre Inocencio's absence and came to a climax a little after the unfortunate incident that put an end to Padre Inocencio's life.

I refer to another dog as huge and ferocious as the one of which I spoke before. This dog belonged to the school. It was a watchdog.

Every day, the moment the classes began in the school, this dog was released into the patio, through which we had to pass in order to reach the stairway which led to the classrooms. The purpose was, I presume, that should we arrive late to the class, the dog would attack and frighten us.

I remember arriving late one day and finding the dog. I remember how my heart sank to my heels. I beheld the door which led to the stairway at the other end of the enormous patio, distant, small and unattainable.

I stood there for a long time, the dog watching me. I thought of circling around the school, but gave up the idea as I knew that there was no other way of reaching the classroom where I was due.

The dog and I remained there for a long time looking at each other. The time was passing and my tardiness increasing. And then I made a resolution. I took some object, I don't know what, and hurled it toward the farthest corner in the patio from the stairway. The dog made for it, and just as he reached it, when he was farthest from the point I wanted to gain, I started at right angles.

It was a mad sprint. I did not run, I flew, swept by uncontrollable panic. I can still hear the air humming in my ears and the dog, who had turned to chase me, was right on my heels. With a final desperate leap, I landed four or five steps on the stairway, past the door where I knew the dog was trained not to enter, and there I remained motionless, stunned by fear, panting from the strain and shock to my nerves.

I arrived very late at my class and the punishment I received on that account seems to me to this day out of all proportion, brutal, cruel beyond adequate description, and I therefore will not attempt to describe it. Perhaps I might be carried too far by my own feelings, feelings which I do not trust, for such was my mental condition in those days that sometimes I fear being unjust. I fear that my imagination enlarges on my experiences; that after all, perhaps things were not as bad nor people as cruel or indifferent as I imagine. For it seems unbelievable that a child of that age could go through so much for such a length of time and older people not know it; that a child could suffer to that extent and older people not offer him a helping hand. Yes, undoubtedly I imagine things worse than they really were.

But I know for one thing that those two dogs of which I have spoken played a great part in the drama of my existence and contributed largely to making those days some of the darkest of my life. They have left an indelible imprint from which I still suffer.

Those two dogs lined my path between school and home. There was a dog closing my way home where I wanted to go, and there was a dog closing my way to school where I had to go. These two animals loomed fatally in my childhood and framed my life, binding it with fear, a fear that woke and brought to the surface feelings that might better have remained dormant and which together with other things made my schooldays more harmful than helpful.

And then the summer . . . a feeling of immense freedom and infinite relief, at home or in the village park, without books, without dogs, without priests. . . ! But my memories of vacation days are confused also, perhaps more so, for it is those things which are unpleasant which remain, due to a self-destroying desire, clearer in our mind or in our flesh. Our memory sometimes seems to pick the unpleasant things out of our past, with masochistic accuracy, and now that summer passes like a cloud gilded with sun, an ephemeral cloud carried away by a hurried wind of time, setting past the horizon of my memories . . . and then the night again. I began the third year of *Bachillerato*.

Things became more entangled. I remember passing through this course without understanding a single word of what I studied. Textbooks out of all proportion to our age. A purely theoretical education beyond our grasp. Priests too ill-tempered or impatient to explain, making us the victims of their personal feelings. Fourteen hours a day of study during a year, and all of them without exception gone to waste. Such is the education which explains the prodigious ignorance of a Spanish graduate.

But going back to the original theme, soon after the school opened we learned that Padre Inocencio had returned bringing with him a young nun from Madrid to the convent next to our school. There was much talk and gossip about the matter in school and out of it. We did not dare to ask Padre Inocencio and he did not seem to care to explain. But the talk went on and our curiosity increased.

One day Alfau came to me:

"Garcia, do you know who the new nun is?"

"No."

"Bejarano's sister. You remember Pepe. Well, her name is Carmen

173

Bejarano, they call her Sister Carmela."

My curiosity knew no limits. We made several conjectures upon the subject. No one had seen her. Alfau had the most absurd ideas regarding the cause of her becoming a nun.

And that same day, I think, we went on the roof of the school and looked down at the convent's grounds.

"You see that one there?"

"Which? That one? Why, that one was here last year."

"No, not that one, the other. You see there by that tree?"

And then I saw her near some trees and up to this day I don't know what I saw in that distant figure that woke something in me.

This term we felt a little happier. We knew that Padre Inocencio had come to stay the whole year and then there were several new things. I may not have learned anything during the classes, but I learned a number of other things. Among others, I learned from Cavañitas that some priests in our school had been seen mounting or perhaps dismounting the convent walls.

"Perhaps to steal some apples," I advanced, and grew indignant because we had been bitterly punished for that same sin.

But Cavañitas winked at Alfau in that way of his that made me feel he was a man of the world and said that it was not for apples they went there. And then he added:

"You had better get wise to it all, Garcia. We are Los Madrileños and must not let this *comehostias* put anything over on us."

The very irreverent way in which Cavañitas had referred to the priests shocked me a little but I was afraid to appear too innocent.

This was at lunch hour and we were in a corner at the patio. Cavañitas drew us closer to him and after looking about furtively began:

"Do you know Padre Mora?"

"Naturally, but what about him?" said I. Alfau seemed to know the story already.

"Well, do you remember the other day, when he told me to stay after the French class?"

"Did you stay after the French class?"

"You probably were half asleep and did not notice it," put in Alfau.

"Probably, but what happened?"

"Well, he sat next to me and put an arm over my shoulder, and then began to say that I was naughty and forward and then—"

Padre Inocencio was coming toward us:

"Well, well, Los Madrileños always together. Come over to the convent with me. I want to present you to Sister Carmela. She is also from Madrid and she is the sister of Pepe. He spoke to her about you and she wants to know how bad you really are." Padre Inocencio laughed. He seemed to be in excellent humor.

Strange to say, I remember the scene that followed as clearly as if it were only yesterday.

I remember that we followed Padre Inocencio to the convent and that we spoke of our studies, but that I knew that my friends were thinking of the same thing I was thinking and that they were possessed of the same curiosity.

I remember that there were two nuns in front of the convent building and that we all said good afternoon to them. And then Padre Inocencio entered the building alone and we were left to wait outside.

While we waited no one of us dared speak first. Such was our expectation that we forgot all about Cavañitas's tale concerning Padre Mora.

I remember that then we saw Padre Inocencio reappear and he was accompanied by a nun. They were walking slowly toward us and they were holding a lively conversation. She talked and laughed cheerfully, moving her hands, acting in a way in which we had seen no other nun act. Padre Inocencio walked beside her, one hand behind and the other playing with the crucifix that hung on his breast, smiling thoughtfully. And I knew that they were not talking about us, that they were talking and thinking of something far more important than we were.

They formed a group so worldly, she was so fresh, so graceful and gay. Padre Inocencio walked with such ease and elegance, with such attentiveness and such a gallant manner, that my thoughts instantly reverted to a young man and young woman whom I had seen once in

Madrid in El Retiro, walking oblivious of everything, in the same style.

And I knew that they were not talking about us, that they were talking and thinking of something far more important than we were. Only once as they approached, she looked, smiled, winked and waved her hand at us. And even then in my incipient masculinity, I felt that it was a feminine concession that she was not like other nuns. When they reached the spot where we stood, Padre Inocencio seemed to wake from a dream.

"Here you have the rascals."

And then we saw that . . . yes, that woman. Her mouth was fresh, with a faint tendency to thickness, her eyes slightly tilted upwards and very black and very bright, and her complexion olive. She seemed very young to be a nun. She was so friendly, her whole body emanated such familiarity, so much informal comradeship, that I thought in her case the name sister very adequate, as the other nuns had always struck me more as a mother-in-law. I told her this once some time after and she laughed, nodded in agreement and called me naughty, giving me a big hug. And then she asked me what I knew about mothers-in-law.

Cavañitas stooped to kiss the edge of her habit, but she held him by the shoulders and kissed him squarely on the mouth. I saw him blush and felt my heart beat quickly. Then she did the same thing with Alfau and myself and then turned to Padre Inocencio and said:

"Nothing for you today."

Padre Inocencio was laughing delightedly. We followed his example, not knowing what else to do in our embarrassment. She spoke quickly and of many things: she spoke of her brother, of the things that Pepito had told her about us, and in the end our embarrassment vanished. We knew we had another friend.

I remember everything as if it were yesterday. I noticed the pleasant smell of cleanliness that came from her, her plumpish hands, her finely polished nails. Decidedly she was not like other nuns.

I remember when she laid her hand on my shoulder and looked at me with mocking seriousness and said I was a little pale. And then she said that she was going to teach us the catechism and told us that she expected us there every Thursday after lunch. And after she had arranged everything she asked Padre Inocencio for his permission.

And, of course, he gave his permission.

When I returned to my classes, I knew I had another friend. Yes, aside from Cavañitas and Alfau, Padre Inocencio and Sister Carmela were my only two friends, the only pleasant things. And I associated that man and that woman intimately, too intimately. They were both exceptional in the Church. Although Padre Inocencio was much older, he had gray hair already, they were both so unusual in that environment, that they became identified in my thoughts. Up to this day I cannot think of one without thinking of the other. But now I know that they were different. Fundamentally, radically different, like a glass of water and a glass of wine.

This second year was not perhaps as bad as the first and Padre Inocencio and Sister Carmela contributed no little to make it more bearable. The lessons with her were one of the sweetest things during that year. All week long we looked forward to them. I remember some of those lessons. I remember when we went over the Ten Commandments and the seven mortal sins. I remember those lessons and that we questioned ourselves, why did she dwell so long upon certain descriptions which were embarrassing to us in her presence? I remember that there was a spark of mischief in her tilted eyes as she dwelt at length upon the sixth commandment and asked us subtle questions one by one. I remember how she dwelt upon those descriptions and that although we did not say so to each other, we liked her much better for it.

I remember how she would offer a big kiss to the one who knew the lesson best and every time she decided that we all knew it just as well. And I remember the day that I stayed after class and she sat beside me and put her arm about my neck. She asked me if I ever thought about sweethearts. Then she was about to ask me something else and Padre Inocencio entered the room and she changed abruptly:

"Padre Inocencio, my greatest trouble is that I like children too much."

Her voice was calm and even, only her breast was undulating quickly. And now I ask myself: was that sheer cynicism, or did she mean it in some other way?

Padre Inocencio looked at her with profound admiration and said: "If that is a trouble, that is my trouble, too."

But there has never been the slightest doubt in my mind as to the meaning of his words. And that day for the first time that man and that woman gave me two different impressions.

Slowly she bored deeply through our hearts. She aroused things in us that were new, she woke new sentiments in us. Like a sweet breeze she blew upon the fire of our imagination and the feelings we entertained toward her were of the strangest and most confused nature. She aroused jealousy in us, she aroused too many things.

Did she delight in playing with children? Did it afford her pleasure to awaken our youthful hearts? Was it wickedness or was it just a weakness? Did what she guessed in us flatter her? The passion of a child must be quite flattering. I know that it must be the sweetest thing.

But was it really so? Perhaps we only imagined it. I have already explained myself. We were so overwrought, we slept so little, we worked so hard, we feared so much, we felt so persecuted. Our minds did not work properly. I think in that school we were all lunatics, we were neurotics. In short, we were *the students,* a bunch of emaciated nervous wrecks.

In describing Sister Carmela's character I prefer not to quote the older people who knew of her. She may have harmed others, but she was good to me and to my friends. Besides, I have always felt that she placed a tacit confidence in us. Sometimes walking with us, she spoke of things that she asked us never to repeat. And yet she always liked to make every individual believe that he was the only one in her thoughts. She was not always sincere and I don't know . . . I don't know. . . . But anyway I can only speak of what I remember happening.

And such was her character to the best of my knowledge:

Sister Carmela was an exceptional nun.

She was enormously attractive.

She was always friendly and gay.

She always wanted to arouse everyone.

She was entirely too human.

And one day she went away.

Although many people said that they expected it, I think it was more or less a surprise to all. To me it was more than a surprise, it was a revelation, which opened my eyes further and left an empty feeling in my soul.

I remember that there was much talk and confusion about it. I remember seeing the boys in circles in the patio of the school and the priests doing their best to break these circles. I remember how the younger students questioned the older ones upon the matter and were left in greater darkness after their complicated explanations. And then I heard my mother discussing it also among some friends who came to the house. She was saying something about a cloud of disgrace hanging over the Bejarano family. I remember hearing the word *incest* for the first time and hearing it often.

I heard someone say that it was bad enough for a nun to elope, but then with her own brother. . . . And the whole village was aroused and there were contrary opinions about the whole thing. Some say that her elder brother had been seen the day before, roaming about the village although they did not know when or how he had arrived, that he had even gone to the convent and had been seen talking to her but that no one suspected anything but a brotherly call. Some other people said that he had not been seen at all. To me everything was confused. All the priests and nuns were in the habit of calling everyone brother and sister and mother and father and I had lost the sense of family relationship to a high degree. I remember thinking that perhaps they spoke of her brother because she was a Sister. . . . In short, I don't know what I thought of the whole thing.

I asked everyone I knew well. I asked my friends, but for once there was something about which Cavañitas and Alfau knew no more than myself. And then one day I spoke to my mother:

"Why do they think it so bad for a nun to take a trip with her own brother? I think it is perfectly all right, don't you?"

My mother looked at me very intently and said slowly:

"Yes, of course. It is not that. It is because some valuables disappeared from the convent chapel and it seems that they took them."

"And is that what they call incest?"

And my mother looked at me still more intently and took a step forward. I drew back as the scene of her coming on a white horse flashed through my mind and then she said:

"Well . . . not precisely," and the tension was released and I feared to ask more.

And then the other thing happened which added so much consternation to the school and the whole village.

Three days after the foregoing incidents, Cavañitas, Alfau and myself were talking in the grounds of the school near the building. We were talking about Sister Carmela and Cavañitas was telling us of something he had heard from some priest. There were other boys and priests about.

Suddenly we heard a thud. I can hear that sound this very moment. It was like a clothesbasket falling on hard pavement, and we turned around and beheld about five yards away something like a dark bundle and a red liquid coming from it.

I still feel the chill I felt that moment. . . . I don't remember who cried first. I know I did not. I was paralyzed. But I heard voices and then some priests came forward and leaned over. The boys rushed up also and the name Padre Inocencio . . . Padre Inocencio . . . Padre Inocencio . . . filled the air carried by every mouth.

And once more, in my mind, I saw my mother advancing rhythmically, fatally on the white horse in time with the cries: Padre Inocencio, Padre Inocencio, Padre Inocencio. . . .

This thing happening suddenly in the middle of our conversation about Sister Carmela created a fearful association between both things. I felt that there was an intimate connection between this sudden death and her elopement. It was such a shock that for an instant I thought and felt with unique clearness.

I knew for a second that the behavior of Sister Carmela must have affected Padre Inocencio as much as it affected me. For a moment I realized what I had felt all along for that extraordinary woman and what I felt I knew that others could feel also and a man more strongly Why these thoughts swept my brain is a thing I do not know. And then I thought I had the key to the dramatic mystery. But now I doubt again

Perhaps it was only my imagination, perhaps the other boys fancied strange things also, as clearly as I thought I did. We had so many shocks in those schooldays, we were so sleepy and tired, we suffered so many hallucinations. I even doubt now what I saw. Perhaps half was reality and half our fancy, perhaps half was a dream and half nightmare. We were pathologic cases, we were mad and insane.

All this happened toward the end of the term. The next day the school was closed and we were told that Padre Inocencio had been the victim of an accident, that, while leaning out of a window, he had suffered a fainting spell and fallen down. But those words carried no weight. Why did they carry no weight? Why did we all know that it had been suicide? Why did we pick the disconnected happenings and weave them into a complete drama? Perhaps it was our childish intuition sharpened by all that suffering, by that maddening constant vigil, by the morbidity which we could not escape. Indeed, we were *the students,* but the problems of life which confronted us were just as puzzling and abstruse as the problems in our classes. They were forced upon us and were too much for our youthful hearts and minds. What we saw from life was as confusing as what we saw in books but more intense and puzzling and dramatic. As it was, it left a deeper track in our spirits and in our flesh and by creating a zone of inattention it helped to make the other things still more foggy.

I need not say how I felt, how we all felt after these last experiences. School became more and more unbearable if possible. I remember the Masses that were sung for the soul of Padre Inocencio as something terribly drowsy through which I invariably went to sleep. I remember that I felt incapable of going through with this life. I remember the overwhelming sleepiness and obsession of those two dogs, growing into a constant panic which maddened me and I felt in my senses that everything was coming to an end soon, that it could not last, that the drama was closing.

And then one day Cavañitas suffered a tremendous punishment. Cavañitas, who was very skilled with the sling, had brought the school dog down with a stone in the head and the dog had to be shot.

That was fate and the first sign of protest which started me into action. When Cavañitas came out from his punishment, I embraced him and told him to let me have a sling.

That night as I went home I held the sling in my hand and carried my *boina* full of stones; of freshly hammered stones, with good sharp edges, just right in size. And I knew that I was almost as good as Cavañitas with the sling, that I seldom missed the mark, and what is more, I knew well that a sling properly used can throw a stone with a terrific force.

That night I was feverish, there was rage in my heart which I have seldom felt afterwards. When I reached the street, I stood at one end and saw it stretch before me, narrow and long. Only a lamp post at the other end. A shadow detached itself from one of the walls and stood in the center. It was the dog and he began to bark.

That had the effect of a lash on me. I remember hearing the sling whiz and a prolonged howl. I was in a paroxysm. I remember the dog receding and I chasing him viciously with one stone after another until I could see the dog no more.

I was possessed of an infernal fury, I felt the blood pounding my temples, and then a window opened and the dog's master appeared and said something about the dog. I cursed him and used the foulest language I had learned. He tried to threaten me and then I slung a stone against his window and followed it with another and the glass clattered down. I remember telling him that I wanted to kill his dog and him, too. And then he went back inside calling me insane and mad, and I think he was right and I ran home.

When they opened the door, I broke down and cried. I don't remember what I said except that I did not intend to study any more or that if I went back to that school I would murder a priest. I cried and cursed and for once was not reprimanded for it. My mother soothed me and told me to be calm and not to fear, that I did not have to study if I did not want to, that I was not going back to school, that I could do what I pleased and sleep as long as I wished. Then I remember her saying something about anemia and she was loving and I felt a great relief and during the days that followed I drank something bitter before meals.

Soon after that we left Vizcaitia and returned to Madrid.

As I have said, everything in those days seems foggy, my brain was in a turmoil. I was very sleepy and tired and had become too high-strung. Now I only see a great confusion and out of that maelstrom of sentiments and ideas, three strange pictures: A woman with her heart pierced by many arrows, a man on a cross, bleeding, with a crown of thorns on his head, and a still more puzzling picture with only a heart aflame. And either my childish intuition or my overwrought imagination of those days found a strange connection between those pictures and a man and a woman whose lives are bound together in my memory by a subtle romantic feeling. . . . All fades then before the dazzling vision of a woman advancing toward me on a great white horse . . . then everything goes black and there are two dogs, two great big dogs, barking in the darkness.

II

Spring

I

My knowledge of the early youth of my friend Garcia is very limited. I know that he was born at the beginning of spring. This is, however, too coincidental a thing to have any bearing upon his case.

Nevertheless, as an infant he was known to be fond of flowers and the sign of anything pertaining to spring brought from him actions and sounds revealing a profound inner delight.

Then came a marked change. I remember him as a boy when we both attended the Colegio de los Padres Salesianos in Vizcaitia. He was pale and thin, with pimpled complexion and a strong tendency to dreaminess and melancholia. These qualities seemed to grow more intense during the spring, a thing which by contrast became more apparent to his companions as we always felt rather happy at the approach of the summer holiday. During these spells, he went about alone and did not mix or play with the other boys.

At first we attributed his attitude to worry about the coming examinations, but later I realized that it must have been due to some other cause as he studied less during those periods and appeared absent-minded and distracted in class, and consistently fell back in his marks.

Then Garcia left Vizcaitia and I did not see him again until I returned to Madrid, where I came in contact with him through mutual acquaintances. It was through these acquaintances that I learned that he wore long hair, wrote poetry and asked his friends for money. Garcia did not work and led an aimless life, a thing in which most of his friends envied him secretly. This, at least, is what I gathered from their comments.

I remember one day in a café, when a friend asked him point-blank:

"Garcia, don't you ever feel a desire to work?"

Garcia was sipping a glass of manzanilla. He finished it without haste and answered:

"Yes, but I do my best to repress it."

From that day my friendship with Garcia was established.

And then, one day I had the first clear glimpse into his life hobby.

We were walking in the Retiro, and I had just become positively aware of the fact that Garcia looked worn out and shabby, exaggeratedly old for his age. His hair was long and quite gray. This was in the month of May.

Garcia was telling me about some poems he was writing or was about to write.

Suddenly, he left my side and advanced ahead. He staggered forth, his head up, his arms stretched in front as if drawn by a vision, and leaned on a big tree.

When I overtook him, there was a strange glow in his face, an expression of infinite joy and happiness which surprised me, and he exclaimed as if finishing our interrupted conversation:

"It is this . . . it is this . . ." and he caressed the tree with a gesture which included the whole scenery. "This eternal season that never fails."

His face contrasted with the sadness of his frame. The day was lukewarm, the air was balmy and all was still. There was a feeling of expectancy. Garcia went on:

"Do you smell those flowers? Can you hear the rustle of the breeze among the foliage? Can you see the lace of light and shadow the trees weave upon the ground?"

My mind told me that all this was secondhand literature and I knew that Garcia always had a lyric way of expressing himself. But I could not rid myself of the poetry of the moment, I felt caught in a trap of sentimentalism and Garcia carried suggestion in his words and in his countenance. He spoke as if in a rapture:

"This is what makes life worth living. Life itself. . . ."

"Yes, El Retiro is very beautiful, it is one of the most poetic parks I have seen." I also wanted to put in a word.

Garcia shook his hand in the air as if wiping my words off an imaginary slate:

"It is not that . . . it is the season, it is this season that never fails. It is this great compensation to all our troubles and disappointments. . . . I have come to depend on nothing else."

There was a pause.

Garcia went on: "You don't know what this means to me. It reconciles me to life every year. It brings me the greatest happiness that I have known. It is what we all hope for, consciously or subconsciously. It is the hope of mankind. Spring means to me what it should mean to you and to everybody, but people seem to go about their business unaware of days like this. They go after petty things and then they are disappointed. They are always hoping for something they think they never can attain, and what they are hoping for is spring, the thing that never fails, the thing on which we can bank everything, the thing to which we should be ever thankful. They do not realize that it is at hand, that it comes to their aid every year. A man may be in misery, he may have no food or no place to sleep. In winter this is hard and he will fear, but then on comes the spring and he fears no more. Spring brings warmth, and fruits and flowers, it brings abundance of life, it brings us safety. . . . But people don't realize this, and they continue to go about with the same cheap winter-providing attitude, oblivious of this great thing that is going on, oblivious of everything important. I feel as if I were the only man who has discovered spring."

"That sounds very nice, but . . ." I was pitifully, or fortunately, failing the situation. I was taking my friend literally and Garcia, still leaning on the tree, signaled me to keep quiet.

"I know all your objections, but, man, don't be ungrateful, spring is here. Do not desecrate the moment. Do not fool yourself; this is the only dependable thing. Everything else passes and fades, but spring always comes."

We were silent a while. Then Garcia said:

"Excuse me," and he embraced the tree.

II

When I left Madrid, Garcia was about to take a position he had secured through the efforts of a good friend. I felt somewhat happy at the thought of leaving Garcia with something safe and to see that he was entering the path of normality and orderly living, for I will not deny that lately I had entertained vague fears about his sanity. I was, however, soon to be disappointed by a letter I received from him which shows that his old ideas had not left him:

"There is a latent poetry in the atmosphere of something vague and distant that is preparing itself, something that is gathering strength and elements to burst forth suddenly, and it is spring, the season which I always await because it brings me happiness. I don't know what there is in spring that I always wait for it and always depend on it as if it were a great resource that never fails. For a long time I have felt this way.

"The other day I was explaining this to Lunarito, the girl who takes care of my room. I told her that upon awaking in the mornings, one could hear something like a distant roar, increasing as a wave that breaks in the sea. I told her that one could hear spring coming and that I have always heard it, that it comes from afar, not only in time but in space. I don't think Lunarito understood me.

"In the mornings one can hear it more clearly, I believe, because one's mind is just awake and more receptive. One's senses are still half asleep and, therefore, more ready to fall under the influence of this element, so great and powerful.

"The balcony of my room is open and I can clearly hear all the noises of the city. But all these things reflect the approaching season and spring vibrates in all of them. There is a strange quality in this season which no other season has. It announces itself beforehand, we feel it in the distance. Luminous, warm days, sprouting in the middle of the winter, bringing us consolation, cheer and hope, like heralds of spring.

"And always at such a time I feel the same vagabond and willful spirit sweeping my conscience and senses, an irresistible desire to throw everything to the devil and seek adventure through the fields, through-out the world. To unite myself to the avalanche of spring and drift with it. . . . Oh, Lord! Without worries of the morrow or unpleasant memories of the past, except perhaps those that are necessary and a bit sad, in order to lend happiness that diaphanous touch of melan-choly which makes it so refined, so perfect, so poetical and so humane. And to be able to jump and roll all over the grass and find that there is an abundance of food and good drink, and all of that which I love. . . . God! If for once things were as one wishes them to be!

"I would work almost with pleasure during the balance of the year if I could abandon myself completely to spring. This would compensate for everything. Of course, it would be much better not to work at all and do nothing but what we like, all year around, but, well . . . well, this season turns my head inside out. It drives me insane with pleasure. My natural dislike for all that which is holy and disagreeable rises to exorbitant proportions. I hear spring coming in the distance, I feel it, I scent it, and I am lost. I execrate everything that smacks of duty, of labor, anything that may bind me. . . . To break all chains and bridles and lunge at full speed, ahead of the earth itself, in order to reach that place of dreams and realities, where spring is eternal. . . !

"But this not being possible, I must content myself with what I have and all these feelings find expression in eruptions like this letter. I must give them some outlet. But at least all of us who have feelings and an aesthetic attitude, somewhat refined; all of us who can hear spring coming in the distance, who are the chosen ones, must dedicate to it a thought every year, some kind of prayer like a tribute of thanks. We must congratulate each other upon its arrival, for notwithstanding the large crop of trouble we reap from life, we can always count on those moments of happiness, which, even if we cannot fully enjoy them, due to circumstances, at least cause our hearts to jump. And this is a great compensation, on this we can always count and it never fails. Bad and disagreeable things pass and fade, but spring always comes.

"I am writing you this because I consider it a duty to share with understanding beings we appreciate and love those things which, due to our subtle intuition, we have discovered to be fountains of joy. To try to share with others would be a disappointment, but you understand me. . . ."

I confess that I did not understand Garcia then, but I think I am beginning to understand now.

III

During the time I was away from Madrid, I did not have news of Garcia regularly. I received a letter from him now and then which always showed a marked decline in his mental faculties. Then I learned that he had given up his position. Some time passed and I returned to Madrid.

I found Garcia living alone in a little house with a garden in the Barrio de Salamanca.

I remember that Lunarito, his maid, opened the door and said that she was glad to see me. I asked after my friend and she told me that Señor Garcia was sick, very sick. That everybody feared for his sanity, that his mind was wandering and he was beginning to have difficulty in recognizing people.

I went upstairs and found Garcia sitting by a balcony, looking out. He seemed to recognize me immediately. He rose and came toward me with outstretched arms and embraced me fondly.

Then I noticed that he had grown fearfully old since I last saw him. He was bent. He wore his hair long as usual, but now it was completely white. Garcia had always walked without resolution as one who has lost his way, but now this characteristic was more noticeable. He almost dragged his feet and seemed to reel. And at that time Garcia could not have been more than thirty years old.

However, he spoke sensibly and with calm. He told me that a relative of his had died and left him some money and this house where he was now.

"Yes," he said, "I am happy here. I have a garden and flowers." He waved at the garden. "Just the kind of place I had always wanted. Peaceful like a mirror reflecting all the seasons of the year. . . . Yes, I am happy."

And I knew that he was not happy.

"Yes, I am happy," he repeated as if he had read my thoughts. "You should see spring here. . . ."

In the quietness of that moment his last sentence went through me like a chill. Here was his mania again, here was the thing that had wrapped itself about his existence. Here was spring.

And then his mind began to wander. He spoke incoherently, in a disconnected manner. I suggested that we go down in the garden, and we went down. This was summer. There were beautiful flower beds and bushes, and the whole garden had an air of abandon which made it densely poetic.

Across the street I discovered a man watering the flowers of his garden. He saw us and waved. I asked Garcia who the gentleman was and Garcia shook his head and sighed:

"The poor fellow. . . . He is a doctor; Dr. José de los Rios." Garcia had assumed a strange expression. "He is . . ." Garcia made a drilling motion with his finger on his temple. "You know? One of the strangest cases I have seen."

At first I believed Garcia and did not know what to say. He was speaking with great seriousness.

"Do you know? Sometimes I have watched him from behind the curtains. He comes out to his garden and performs strange things. I saw him one day talk to the flowers and then he began to dance and all the flowers beat time for him."

Now I knew and tried to soothe Garcia, but he was strong on the subject of his neighbor.

"He seems to have an uncanny power upon nature. He has a little cane with which he performs all his tricks and once I saw him plant the cane in the ground and the cane grew and flourished like a tree."

I tried to distract Garcia, to change the conversation, but he insisted with that eagerness peculiar to such cases:

"Yes. Another day I saw him at El Retiro. He did not see me and I followed him at a distance. And do you know what he did? He had that little cane of his and he tapped the trees there with it. Then he produced a stethoscope and applied it to a tree as if he were listening to its heart, and then he would shake his head and approach another tree and repeat the same operation. I overtook him and arrived in time to hear him say:

" 'The spring is not coming this year. I cannot hear it.'

"Well, that lack of faith made me indignant. I addressed him and he seemed to be in great confusion. And then I told him that I always heard the spring without the aid of such devices, that I could hear spring in everything, yes, in everything . . . that he could never hear it through that apparatus and that it took a poet and not a doctor to sense the approaching of spring. I told him that he was insane to doubt that it was coming, that other things may fail, but spring . . . always . . . comes. . . ."

Garcia's voice broke here and he hung his head as if with deep resignation under the fatality of that last statement which sounded cruelly ominous. I could not stand that much longer. I made a last effort to change the course of conversation:

"Calm yourself, Garcia; you are a happy man. You said so yourself. I was just thinking how happy you must be in this beautiful garden. . . ."

He looked at me as if he did not understand what I was saying, almost as if he did not know who I was. And then he turned and walked away from me. He staggered forth, his arms stretched in front as if drawn by that eternal vision.

I followed. He stopped before a bush that was in full bloom and caressed the flowers and the leaves with trembling hands, with hungry eyes melting in tears. At last he held two branches and pressed them tightly. He was shaking all over and looked at me profoundly as if seeking understanding and sympathy. I approached him, but he held me away with a hand.

"It is this . . . it is this. . . ."

I knew he was trying to find the words that could express his feelings, but I knew that there could be no such words, and I nodded to him my understanding.

There came a grateful look into his eyes and for a long time we remained silent.

Then Garcia said:

"Excuse me," and he wept.

IV

One day I went to call on Garcia and found his house closed and nobody answered my bell. Dr. José de los Rios was across the street in his garden and I inquired of him. He came over and told me of the sad incident which had taken place during my absence.

It was toward the end of the winter. It seems that during the days previous to this happening, Garcia had remained in his room, the windows and door shut. This Dr. de los Rios had gathered from the explanations of Lunarito, who was the only person who had seen Garcia at the time, when she brought him something to eat.

Then one day Dr. de los Rios, who was as usual in his garden, saw Garcia rush out of his front door; he saw him throw the garden gate open and run down the street yelling:

"Spring is coming . . . ! Spring is coming . . . !"

Dr. de los Rios followed him and found him farther down the street, surrounded by people who were trying to calm him and children who mocked him. Dr. de los Rios took him home and administered some drug, and it was the doctor who afterwards took Garcia to the insane asylum.

And I thought:

So it was Dr. de los Rios, the man whom Garcia had accused of insanity, the same man whose sanity I had doubted for a moment, who had finally taken my friend to the asylum. And I kept on thinking about the strange irony of life while Dr. José de los Rios explained to me the case of Garcia.

According to him, it was a case of temporary insanity and he did not doubt that with the proper treatment my friend could recover permanently. Dr. de los Rios spoke of nervous disorders, of their causes and effects. He mentioned weakening of the spine and then commented on bad habits. But he spoke without the slightest shade of moralizing.

I received the impression that he had been watching over Garcia for some time and that Garcia had confided in him. I also received a pleasant impression from Dr. de los Rios. His whole personality was very agreeable. He was a man who created the impression of being clear physically and mentally. His eyes were blue, his hair and pointed beard as well as his mustache blond, and his complexion fair. He spoke with a quiet voice and air, and also with precision free from pedantry. I liked Dr. José de los Rios very much and should like to dedicate a chapter or two to him, but will leave that for a better occasion.

Dr. de los Rios was right. Garcia only suffered temporary insanity. He spent only one year at the asylum and was released.

When Garcia returned to his house I called on him. I had lacked the courage to visit him at the asylum. Another sad blow awaited me. I remember that Lunarito led the way upstairs and that I saw Garcia sitting by the balcony in his room, in exactly the same position in which I had seen him the last time. But this time he did not rise to meet me. Lunarito led him by the hand to me and then I discovered that he was blind.

My feelings are easy to imagine. I had already grown so fond of Garcia . . . ! We embraced each other long and tightly and I stroked his white head but made no comments.

And then I noticed another novelty: two huge mastiff dogs who made their entrance silently into the room and stood at both sides of the chair where Garcia sat, after our greetings. I have forgotten to mention that Garcia all his life had experienced a mixture of fear and repugnance toward dogs that was one of the most marked features of his character. I was consequently greatly surprised at the appearance of these two magnificent specimens of the canine family, whom Garcia seemed to treat with decided friendliness.

I remember my friend's speech and I can still hear his resigned voice:

"That whole year of darkness . . . like a void in my existence of which I hardly remember a thing. And then to recover my reason only to be more conscious of this new misfortune, of this new darkness from which I shall never emerge. . . . Can you realize it?"

And I did not think I could.

Garcia continued, lowering his voice, pursuing his idea like a man obsessed:

"Yes, that year . . . that year was only the end of a longer drama, of my whole past life that was fortunately . . . or unfortunately . . . torn from me completely. Looking back now, it seems as if my whole existence belonged to some other being, a being whose life was a continuous internal storm and an external farce. Yes, during that year in which my mind went to sleep I feel that my whole being was substituted. I have no recollections in detail but I have vague and great subconscious feelings that terrible things took place, things that no man alive, mentally awake, could bear to see, much less experience. . . . Yes, my whole past life was torn from me. I have been born again, nothing remains from that, nothing except one thing, a thing that is eternal, a thing . . ."

I stood up:

"Stop, Garcia . . . don't say it. I know what thing that is."

"Yes . . . only that thing."

My friend's voice was now still lower and concentrated like a coarse whisper. The two dogs were rubbing their heads on his sides.

"I wish I had never recovered my reason, because it is so painful to look back into one's own life and see it clearly. Since my childhood that love for my mother, that assumed proportions which later frightened me. . . . To live up to her slightest wishes, to live only for her. . . . Do you understand me? . . ."

I had slowly receded from Garcia but he had not noticed it and his voice had grown lower, dimmer. The dogs had grown restless and noisy, I could hear no more for a while. When I approached Garcia again he was finishing:

"... which every year came with the spring and never left me, until I came to fear that season that became associated with my whole life. And it was maddening to think I could not check its pace, to know that it was ominously advancing to destroy me, to know that it never fails, that there is no hope, that spring always comes."

When I left Garcia it was quite dark and as I walked down the street, I heard the two dogs barking for a long time.

V

One day I took Garcia for a walk in El Retiro. It was again the month of May. We were silent, Garcia held my arm and leaned on a cane. He said after a while:

"Let us sit down and then tell me all about the day. You know I cannot see it."

We sat down on a bench, and I did not know what to say.

"It is very bright today, Garcia. . . . The sky is blue . . . you know the sky of Madrid. . . ."

"Yes, I remember it. I can see it within me. Yes, how blue it is!"

"Yes, very blue, Garcia, and the sun is bright. . . ."

"Naturally, when the sky is blue, the sun is usually bright."

"El Retiro is the same as ever. You remember it. . . . The same flower beds, the same shadowy paths. . . . You remember El Retiro. . . ."

Garcia signaled me to keep quiet:

"I can feel everything, I can sense it all better than you or anyone can tell me. Stop. The day itself is talking to me. I can feel the sun, I can smell the flowers and hear the wind in the trees. . . . I can feel everything. The day talks to the blind and it is talking to me now. Be silent, let me listen. . . ."

And I was silent and Garcia bent his head. I saw the sun upon his broken frame, on his white head. His face was all attention, he did not move and he was listening, listening. . . .

195

Suddenly he stood up and advanced. He staggered forth, his head up, the sun upon his sightless eyes, his arms stretched in front as if drawn by his eternal vision.

I followed him and remembered the first day I saw him walk in that manner, as if he could see nothing but his own inner dream. All those actions of the past pointed at this sad realization, at this day when he could see no more the thing he had loved so, the day, the light, the spring.

Garcia leaned on a big tree and felt me near.

"It is this . . . it is this. . . ."

"I understand, Garcia."

We were silent a while. Then he said:

"Excuse me," and nothing more.

VI

One morning in March, Lunarito came to my house. She told me that her master was very sick and wanted to see me.

When I arrived I found Garcia in bed. He was extremely thin, he looked almost like a corpse. His voice sounded weak.

"Bad friend," he said, "I could have died and you would not have known it. I have been very sick all winter and you never came to see me."

I protested that my occupation had kept me away and that I did not know that he was sick.

"Yes. I have been very sick and I am still more sick now. I don't know what is the matter with me. Perhaps something wrong with the heart. The doctor says that as long as the cold weather lasts I will be all right, but then . . . the warm weather will soon come . . . you know it always comes . . . and I fear it."

I remained a while with Garcia, telling him that he would recover and trying to cheer him up, but when I left him, there was hopelessness in his face. I promised to return next week.

I returned on the twenty-first of March and found Garcia looking, if possible, still worse. He was lying on the pillows and his blind eyes were fixed on a balcony that faced him. The two dogs were standing at the side of the bed as if ready to defend their master.

I sat down by him and held one of his hands; it was quite cold. Then he spoke:

"It is that fear of the inevitable. . . . Spring is almost here now, and I know that I will die. The doctor said so, I forced it out of Lunarito. . . . To know that I must die, that I cannot stop that season, that it is advancing, that there is no hope. . . . Spring and my life have become strangely blended. Spring has been to me like a lover. I have bound my destiny to it, it has brought me happiness and sorrow, and now it brings me death. . . . To think that the season which brings life to all will come to kill me, to know that it is eternal, that it will go on forever and I shall not see it again. I loved it so much! And now I fear it as I did in my youth. . . . At least if I were sure that when I die I shall be freed from the fatality of a thing that always comes, that never fails. If I were sure of eternal rest undisturbed by that distant humming of the approaching spring . . ."

The two dogs stood motionless at the sides of the bed like the statues of a sepulcher, one of them almost touching my sleeve. Garcia was speaking excitedly. I tried to soothe him. He went on:

"But perhaps the dead do not rest, perhaps they wake up when a sea of dirt breaks through the torn boards of their wrecked coffin. Perhaps under the ground they will be more intimately blended with life and will feel its reactions more directly. . . . They will have strange hallucinations, they will have vague reminiscences of their past life. They will dream that they are alive, they will dream about the sun of luminous days. . . . Under the ground, among the roots of trees, they will feel more than ever . . . they will hear the fatal roar, they will hear the dreaded roar . . . they will hear the increasing roar of the approaching spring. . . ."

It was quite dark now and the two animals were restless, they lifted their heads, pointed their ears and sniffed.

"Perhaps it will come from afar, like a seismic tremor, like an undulation shaking them in more plastic and intense dreams. . . . They will hear spring coming at full gallop and then they will shudder, because they are going to witness for the first time and clearer than ever, with all its secrets, with all its charms and naked, the eternal scene of eternal life. . . ."

Garcia was like a man under a strong hallucination. He sat up in the bed and his sightless eyes seemed to have found at last the vision which had drawn him all his life, a vision clear and dazzling in his blindness.

I should have tried to soothe him, but he held me spellbound with the power of his strange suggestion. I sat back by him with a mixture of fear and great sadness as he went on, almost in a paroxysm:

"Yes . . . in their shadows . . . they will see it then like a picture full of light and color upon a dark mirror . . . within the emptiness of their skull . . . in that dark chamber it will be reflected . . . and then they will see spring riding upon a white unbridled horse, with a helmet of sun melting into thick tresses over a great green robe and an infinite force of creation. They will see life, that comes to wake and drag them forth, and they will hope. . . . One being will die and then another, but that is not the triumph of death . . . life goes on. . . . Spring comes. . . . Spring always comes . . . !"

The two dogs seemed to be no longer able to restrain themselves and began to howl intermittently. Garcia continued:

"In their emotion they will rise. . . . Upon feeling the germ of life they will rise to find themselves blind, to find themselves dumb, to find themselves deaf, to find themselves dead. . . . They will revive within four boards with their senses clogged with dirt . . . and then the last thing will be dead in them . . . then hope will be dead. . . . They will find themselves coming back to life in a repugnant and horrible fashion, in an impersonal way. . . . The dream of life has passed through them for the last time, leaving them a helpless heap of worms. . . .

"And they will see spring receding and will find it again in a tree, or in a flower, or in something else. . . . Everything is alike, all is eternal. . . . With the same unconscious optimism life goes on, spring comes. . . . Spring always comes. . . . Spring . . . always . . . comes!"

Garcia sank back exhausted in his pillows. The whole room was now submerged in deep shadows and there were two dogs, two great big dogs, howling in the darkness.

VII

I returned one week after. I felt that I was calling on Garcia for the last time. Lunarito opened the door for me and then closed it carefully behind. The house was silent. At the door of my friend's chamber I met Dr. de los Rios coming out.

"He is in very bad shape," he said. "He may die any moment now. I don't think he will even live until noontime." His calm voice was more veiled than usual. I made no answer.

"Yes, there is no hope now . . . a whole degeneration of the system." His clear eyes looked at me searchingly. "You know his mania, don't you?"

"Yes, I know it."

Dr. de los Rios looked distractedly through me, beyond me.

"Well . . ." he said. He shook my hand and departed.

I found Garcia in a pitiful condition. He was breathing with difficulty. His head was thrown back on the pillows and his blind eyes were sunken.

The curtains were drawn and the room was in shadow. I looked around but did not see the dogs.

Garcia recognized my step. His intuition seemed sharpened by the approach of death. He turned his head toward me and there was eagerness in his expression.

"Did you close the door when you came in?" His voice was almost inaudible and accompanied by a whistling.

"Yes. Lunarito closed it." He seemed relieved.

"For three days I have had all balconies and doors closed. I am keeping the enemy away. . . . Spring has been here three days already. . . . It has come to get me, but I do not let it enter. . . . I keep all balconies and doors shut. . . . It is a real siege. . . .

"Three days spring has been hovering around . . . roaming about the house, right outside the balconies, trying to push its way in. . . . There it goes now. . . . Can you hear it crackling? Can you hear it humming? Can you hear its reinforcements approaching? Listen . . . listen . . . !"

I remained silent. Instinctively I listened. And that moment I heard in the distance the sound of horses' hoofs upon the pavement, they were approaching . . . and soon a carriage passed by the street and I heard young and cheerful voices. And then the sound of the whole city outside, the sound of life and nature.

Garcia dropped the hand which he had raised. A great relaxation had come over his countenance. He looked infinitely tired and resigned.

"Three days of this. . . . It is no use. One cannot hold out against such a foe. . . . Life is stronger than man. . . . It is no use. I must give in." He made a last effort to lift himself and turned toward me. "Let us end it now. . . . I am choking. . . . Go, go open that window. . . ."

Mechanically I moved, I felt that every limb in me acted regardless of my will. I threw the curtains aside and a stream of light inundated the room. . . . Then I lifted the hook and flung the window open. . . .

Spring came in.

Afterword

Fifty-two years ago, on June 27, 1936, I reviewed a book in the *Nation.*
Very favorably. The author, Felipe Alfau, was said to be a young Spaniard
writing in English. Spain was Republican then; the Franco revolt that
turned into the Spanish Civil War began on July 19, three weeks and a
day later. The charm exercised on me by *Locos,* therefore, cannot have
been a matter of politics. And I was ignorant of Spain and Spanish. It
was more like love. I was enamored of that book and never forgot it,
though my memory of it, I now perceive on rereading, is somewhat
distorted, as of an excited young love affair. Alfau, or his book, was
evidently my fatal type, which I would meet again in Vladimir
Nabokov's *Pale Fire* and more than once in Italo Calvino. But *Locos* was
the first. And it appears to have been the author's unique book, fittingly,
as it were. I never heard of Alfau again, though for a time I used to ask
about him whenever I met a Spaniard; not one knew his name. Maybe
that was because he lived in the United States, if indeed he did. But in
this country I never found anyone besides me who had read *Locos.*
Now the book is being reissued. Launched more than fifty years ago by
a Farrar and Rinehart club of so-called "Discoverers," it has been re-
discovered, by what means I don't know.

To come back to it has been a bit eerie, at least on first sight—a cross
between recognition and non-recognition. For example, what has
stuck in my memory is a lengthy account of a police convention in
Madrid that coincided merrily with a crime wave, the one giving rise to
the other: crooks converged on the city, free to practice their trade
while the police attended panel discussions and lectures on criminality. Well, it would be too much to say that none of that is in *Locos;* it
is there but in the space of a few sentences and as a mere suggestion.

The fifth chapter, "The Wallet," begins: "During the 19— police
convention at Madrid, a very unfortunate occurrence took place.
Something went wrong with the lighting system of the city and the
whole metropolis was left in complete darkness." It is the power failure

that offers the assembled criminals their opportunity. "It was a most deplorable thing, for it coincided with the undesirable immigration of a regular herd of international crooks who since the beginning of the World War had migrated into Spain and now cooperated with resident crooks in a most energetic manner. . . . As if all these people had been waiting for that rare opportunity, the moment the lights went out in Madrid, thieves, gunmen, holdup men, pickpockets, in short all the members of the outlaw family, sprang up in every corner as though by enchantment." Then: ". . . it came to pass that during the Police Convention of 19—, Madrid had a criminal convention as well. Of course, the police were bestowing all their efforts and time upon discussing matters of regulation, discipline and now and then how to improve the method of hunting criminals . . . and naturally, after each session . . . had neither time nor energy to put a check to the outrages. . . . Therefore all crooks felt safer and freer to perform their duty in Madrid, where the cream of the police were gathered, than anywhere else."

That is all, a preamble. The body of the chapter has to do with the stolen wallet of the Prefect of Police. The power failure, which provides a realistic explanation, had slipped my memory, and I was left with the delightful illogic—or logic—of parallel conventions of police and criminals. The purest Alfau, a distillate.

"The Wallet," actually, may be the center of the book, whose subject is Spain regarded as an absurdity, a compound of beggars, pimps, policemen, nuns, thieves, priests, murderers, confidence artists. The title, meaning "The Crazies," refers to a Café de los Locos in Toledo, where in the first chapter virtually all the principal characters are introduced as habitués suited to be "characters" for the bad fiction writers who, like the author, drop in to observe them. There are Dr. de los Rios, the medical attendant of most of the human wreckage washed up at those tables; Gaston Bejarano, a pimp known as El Cogote; Don Laureano Baez, a well-to-do professional beggar; his maid/daughter Lunarito, Sister Carmela, who is the same as Carmen, a runaway nun; Garcia, a poet who becomes a fingerprint expert; Padre Inocencio, a Salesian monk; Don Benito, the Prefect of Police; Felipe Alfau; Don Gil

Bejarano, a junk dealer, uncle of El Cogote; Pepe Bejarano, a good-looking young man, brother of El Cogote; Doña Micaela Valverde, a triple widow and necrophile.

Only missing is the highly significant Señor Olózaga, at one time known as the Black Mandarin, a giant, former galley slave, baptized and brought up by Spanish monks in China, former butterfly charmer in a circus, former potentate in the Spanish Philippines, now running a bizarre agency for the collection of delinquent debts and another for buying and selling dead people's clothes. But he is connected with the other "characters" of the Café de los Locos both in his own right and by marriage to Tía Mariquita, his fifth wife, who lives in a house that coughs—their secretary, mistaken for her husband, is murdered by Don Laureano Baez and his daughter/maid Lunarito—one of many cases of mistaken identity. As the Black Mandarin in the Philippines, he has sought the hand of the blue-eyed daughter of Don Esteban Bejarano y Ulloa, a Spanish official, and been rejected because of his color. This, precisely, was the father of Don Gil Bejarano (see above), the brother-in-law of the Prefect of Police and inventor of a theory of fingerprints, which pops up in Chapter 4, where, incidentally, we find Padre Inocencio playing cards with the Bejarano family while the young daughter, Carmen, is having sex with her brother Gaston.

Such underground—or underworld—links are characteristic and combine with the rather giddy mutability displayed by the characters. Lunarito is Carmen, who is going to be Sister Carmela; at one point we find her married to El Cogote, none other than her brother Gaston, who cannot, of course, *be* her brother if she is the daughter of the beggar, Don Laureano Baez. And yet Don Laureano's wife, when we are introduced to him as the bartender of the Café de los Locos, is Felisa, which is the name of Carmen's mother, the sister of Don Benito, the Prefect of Police. . . . In the Prologue, and occasionally thereafter, the author makes a great point of the uncontrollability of his characters, but this familiar notion (as in "Falstaff got away from Shakespeare") is the least interesting feature. The changing and interchanging of the people, resembling "shot" silk, has no need of the whimsy of a loss of auctorial control. If any aspect of the book has aged, it is this whimsicality.

It is not only the characters of *Locos* that have that queer shimmer or iridescence. Place and time are subject to it as well. A fact I think I missed back in 1936 is the discrepancy between the location of the Café de los Locos—Toledo—where the "characters" are gathered for inspection, and their actual residence—Madrid. What are these Madrileños doing in Toledo? I suppose it must be because of the reputation of Toledo as a mad, fantastic city, a myth, a city, as Alfau says, that "died in the Renaissance"; he speaks of "Toledo on its hill . . . like a petrified forest of centuries." The city that died in the Renaissance and lives on, petrified, can of course figure as an image of Spain. One more quotation may be relevant to the underlying theme of impersonation as a national trait: "the action of this book develops mainly in Spain, a land in which not the thought nor the word, but the action with a meaning—the gesture—has grown into a national specialty. . . ."

Spain and its former possessions—Cuba and the Philippines—constitute the scene; their obverse is China, for a Spaniard the other end of the world, and here the provenance of Señor Olózaga, baptized "Juan Chinelato" by the bearded, tobacco-smoking monks who raised him.

One thing that certainly escaped me as a young reviewer is the hidden presence of this "Juan Chinelato" in the first chapter, the one called "Identity" and laid in the Café of the Crazies. He is there in the form of a little Chinese figure made of porcelain being hawked by Don Gil Bejarano in his character of junk dealer. "Don Gil approached us," writes Alfau. " 'Here is a real bargain,' he said, tossing the porcelain figure on the palm of his hand. 'It is a real old work of art made in China. What do you say?' I looked at the figure which was delicately made. It represented a herculean warrior with drooping mustache and a ferocious expression. He had a butterfly on his shoulder. The color of the face was not yellow but a darker color, more like bronze. . . . 'Perhaps it is not Chinese but Indian.' Don Gil . . . looked slightly annoyed. 'No, it is Chinese,' he said." And he continues to praise it: " 'Yes, this is a real Chinese mandarin or warrior, I don't know which, and it is a real bargain.' " A minute later, thanks to an inadvertent movement, the figure is smashed to pieces on the marble-topped café table.

This is a beautifully constructed book and full of surprises. Another example: one does not notice in this opening chapter the unusually small hand of Don Gil, seen only as a mark on a whitewashed wall. The lightly dropped hint is picked up unobtrusively like a palmed coin several chapters later when Don Gil is being arrested at the reluctant order of his brother-in-law because his fingerprints have been found all over the scene of a crime: "Don Gil had very small hands . . . and the handcuffs did not fit securely enough. . . . 'Officer, those handcuffs are too big for me. You had better get a rope or something.' " In his conversations with the Prefect, he has kept working "the man from China," that is, the man who has the perfect alibi but is tracked down by science through the prints his hands have left. His last article, published in a Madrid newspaper on the day of his apprehension, is entitled "Fingerprints, a sure antidote against all alibis," and his last words, which he keeps reiterating as he is carried off in the police wagon, are "I am the man from China. . . . Fingerprints never fail."

Perhaps police work and criminality, just as much as mad, fantastic Spain, are the subject of *Locos*. And considerable detection is required on the reader's part, to be repaid, as in the hunt for "Wanted" law-breakers, with a handsome reward. For instance, among the clues planted to the mute presence of Señor Olózaga in the Café of the Crazies there is simply the word "butterfly"; I failed to catch the signal until the third reading. And I still have a lot of sleuthing to do on Carmen-Carmela-Lunarito and the beauty spot on Lunarito's body that she charges a fee to show. A knowledge of Spanish might help. In the Spanish light, each figure is dogged by a shadow, like a spy or tailing detective, though sometimes the long shadow is ahead: "She stood at the end of her own shadow against the far diffused light of the corner lamp post and there was something ominous in that." It may be that this is the link between the theme of Spain and the theme of the criminal with his attendant policeman. In some moods *Locos* could be classed as "luminist" fiction. But I must leave some work (which translates into pleasure) for the reader.

If *Locos* is, or was, my fatal type, what I fell in love with, all unknow-ing, was the modernist novel as detective story. There is detective work, surely, supplied by Nabokov for the reader of *Pale Fire*. I mentioned Calvino, too, but there is another, quite recent example, which I nearly overlooked. *The Name of the Rose,* of course. It is not only a detective story in itself but it also contains an allusion to Sherlock Holmes and *The Hound of the Baskervilles*. But in *Locos* Sherlock Holmes is already present: while in England Pepe Bejarano pretends to have studied under him, which explains his uncanny ability to recover his uncle, the Prefect's, wallet. The grateful police officer, who does not know whether Conan Doyle's creation is a real person or not, wants to express his thanks. " 'Yes, Pepe, yes. I should like to write an official letter to that gentleman, to that great man—Cherlomsky, is that the name?' "

Yes, there is a family resemblance to Nabokov, to Calvino, to Eco. And perhaps, though I cannot vouch for it, to Borges, too.

Mary McCarthy

DALKEY ARCHIVE PAPERBACKS

DALKEY ARCHIVE PAPERBACKS

Dalkey Archive Press, ISU Box 4241, Normal, IL 61790–4241

fax (309) 438–7422

Visit our website at www.cas.ilstu.edu/english/dalkey/dalkey.html